DEATH TRAP ON THE PLATTE

1

Vance Jardine swung his horse off the stage road into a pack trail which cut through the brushy hills and shortened the distance to Del Rosa by half a mile. It had been two years since he had followed this route, but it was as though he had followed it only yesterday. Each turn, each ascent along the narrow saddle path was unchanged, engraved on his mind since boyhood.

He ducked the overhanging branches of live oak, and occasionally hiked his long legs onto the saddlehorn in the squeezes where the trail crowded between boulders and trees. Small lizards sped to cover, elusive shadows underfoot. A road-runner, its long tail kited, raced along the hoof-beaten path, swerved into the brush and was gone. Wind and sun had blurred the pad tracks left by a night-prowling bobcat. Javelinas had cut sharp hoofprints in the cool of dawn.

It was now afternoon and he welcomed the harsh, dry hand of the sun. He pulled off his hat and let the warm wind finger through his hair. It was very dark in hue and had grown to respectable length in a month's time from the skin-short cropping that had been its style for two years. He had feared that it might have turned gray, for he had seen other men take on the sterile, lifeless hue of the stone walls that had been his world.

He had been spared that, at least, even though he felt far older than his twenty-seven years. But he was free, at last.

He looked up at the hot sky. "How sweet you are," he said aloud. He spoke to the wind. "How good you smell."

The trail carried him to the backbone of a ridge and he glimpsed Del Rosa town, nestled among the scattered oaks along Armadillo Creek.

His home town. "And if any one of 'em looks crossways at me, or high-chins me, I'll hit him in the nose," he said, and laughed.

He became aware of the clatter of overtaking hoofs. More than one rider was approaching on the trail, still hidden by the brush. His horse, which already had more than thirty miles under its hoofs for the day, was plodding in heavy going along the bed of a small coulee so narrow its clay walls, saddle-high, brushed his stirrups.

He glanced over his shoulder as two riders, their horses at a full gallop, charged into the coulee back of him. One was a young woman riding sidesaddle on a fine bay gelding. Following in the dust her horse kicked up was a leathery vaquero with the fierce dark features of a Yaqui. Juan Sonora was growing gray and seamed, but his obsidian eyes still held the eagle look.

The young woman was forced to yank the

gelding to a sliding stop to avoid running Vance down. The gelding, strong and high-bred, reared, pawing the air, trying to unseat its rider. Although taken by surprise and handicapped by a heavy, fashionable riding skirt, she sat out the storm with confidence and brought the horse under stern control.

She straightened her English-style derby hat with the loop of her riding crop and spoke to the horse. "Damn your blasted hide, Rebel, if you try again to pile me I'll tan you for fair, you hear me?"

She glared at Vance with brown eyes that were very lively, very imperious. "Hurry!" she exclaimed. "Gig that turtle you're riding, or do I have to jump this bay right over your slowpoke head."

"That," Vance said, "I'd like to see."

"Haven't you heard?" she cried. "They've sold the pool cattle! The whole herd! They're coming home with nearly a hundred thousand dollars! In cash money! In gold! Gold for everybody. Everybody's on their way to town to celebrate!"

"I don't know what you're talking about," Vance said, "but that's something else I'd like to see. A hundred thousand dollars in gold would make quite a glitter. It'd be a sight as eye-popping as you jumping a horse over my hat."

"Hurry, I say!" she raged. "Or I'll lay a whip on that crow-bait you're riding. I'll—"

Then she recognized him. She sat, holding

9

a tight rein on the bay, measuring him with the curiosity one would have for a rare and potentially dangerous specimen.

"Well!" she said. Her eyes turned dark amber and she frowned as though the day was suddenly marred. She had an interesting face, with a good mouth and a nose that was slightly tilted as though she wanted him to know he was inferior. Her cheekbones were high, her fingers slender and well-kept. She had a white silk scarf knotted about her throat.

For a moment she hesitated, and hesitation had never been one of Anastasia Fitzroy's qualities. Then she forced her mount closer and raised the riding crop to make good her threat of belting Vance's horse.

He reached out, caught her arm, holding the crop poised. "You spoiled brat!" he said. "If you want to pass me, wait your turn. You'll get a chance soon. The trail widens ahead—as you well know."

The Yaqui rode close, a six-shooter drawn. Vance eyed him. Juan Sonora did not cock the weapon. Instead, he lowered it. He had been Stacy Fitzroy's bodyguard from the time she had left the cradle. His craggy face offered no change of expression, but Vance believed there was a twinkle of amusement in his keen eyes— and perhaps even a note of approval.

Stacy Fitzroy had been raised to be a lady and

a snob. Nevertheless, there was in her the rowdy toughness to resist and to test his strength. She was far from being a weakling, but it was an unequal contest, for he had spent the biggest part of the past two years swinging a jackhammer on a drill at the prison quarry.

She said, "Blast you! You never change, do you? Let go of me!"

He released her arm, and disdainfully eyed the riding crop. "If you ever hit an honest cowhorse with that thing, and he found it out, he'd be mighty insulted," he said. "After this, carry a quirt like all good Texans do."

"That I will," she said. "And I won't bother on using it on a horse when the likes of you are around. Get out of my way!"

"Tut, tut!" Vance said. "I see the Fitzroys are as nasty-tempered as ever. You can pass when there's room. Follow me."

"You—you jailb—! You outlaw!"

He stirred his horse into motion. "Jailbird is what you started to call me. Not any longer. I'm out. I'm even a citizen again. A full pardon. Signed by the governor."

"So I heard," Stacy Fitzroy said. "But nobody dreamed you'd have the brass to come back to Del Rosa."

"Being as the Jardines were in this range as long as the Fitzroys, I sort of feel like I belong here," he said.

His horse emerged from the coulee, offering her the chance to push past him. In doing so she crowded the gelding roughly against his mount, jostling it almost to its knees. Without glancing back she spurred her mount again into a gallop.

Juan Sonora rode by with more care. "*Gracias, señor*," he said. He added in a murmur, "It is like it was when you two were tadpoles, is it not? Even then the flint and steel struck fire." He rode on in pursuit of Stacy Fitzroy.

"Next time," Vance assured his horse, "I'll carry with me a paddle and give her what she's been needing for a long, long time. And in the right place."

He knew it wasn't likely their paths would cross very often. They had been schoolchildren together, but their stations in life had veered far apart as they had grown to maturity. He was surprised she had even acknowledged she knew him.

She had been born with the proverbial gold spoon in her mouth at Oak Hill, her father's pretentious ranch house where only the important visitors were privileged to enter by the big, carved front door. Vance had never entered the Fitzroy mansion by either the front or any other door. Nor any Jardine, for that matter. Major Webster Fitzroy had never given any sign he knew of the existence of the gambling, hard-riding, boisterous Jardines, whose way of life was at such odds with his scheme of things.

Stacy Fitzroy was an only child. Her mother, a handsome woman, who presided over Oak Hill's social affairs, addressed her daughter by her given name, Anastasia, but she was Stacy Fitzroy to everyone else in the Del Rosa country. Stacy Fitz was a common designation. The name was never used in a commonplace manner. Sometimes it was uttered in derision—another term for envy—sometimes in wonder, sometimes in reluctant admiration.

She was the most dashingly attractive girl in the Del Rosa. The best horsewoman. In fact, many men could not stay with her in riding to hounds, or spearing javelinas. Few tried to match her recklessness.

She had been educated at expensive Eastern schools, with the finishing touches put on in Europe. The fashionable riding habit, the derby, the jockey boots were, no doubt, affectations of the moment. Stacy Fitzroy often set feminine tongues going by appearing in the very latest mode.

She had other ways of rubbing the fur in the wrong direction—Vance's in particular. As schoolchildren, she had gone out of her way to patronize him and make it clear he was hardly worth even being looked down on.

This latest encounter seemed to indicate that if she had changed, it was for the worse. Still, it was obvious she had been impelled by great excitement. Even Stacy Fitzroy, with all her belief that she was privileged to ride rough-shod over lesser mortals, had never attempted such tactics with a Jardine, and with Vance in particular.

He angrily tried to stir his horse to a faster gait with the urge to overtake her. Just what he might do if he succeeded, he had no idea. He abandoned the notion in the next instant. For one thing, his mount could never hope to catch the bay gelding. He had paid forty-four dollars for the animal in the auction ring at San Antonio. Like the secondhand saddle he was riding, it had its limitations.

For another thing, he would have to eat dust if he attempted what was sure to be a losing race, for the spume the two horses had kicked up hung thick in the hot air. He let his mount plod along until this nuisance had faded.

The trail carried him to another rise from which he had a closer view of the sprawl of adobe and frame structures that formed Del Rosa. The stores were clustered along a block or two of Sam Houston Street. The few saloons and gambling houses were on Alamo Street. Goatyards and mule corrals fringed the settlement.

Del Rosa had seen its ups and downs. It had skyrocketed brilliantly in the early days of trail driving and had flamed out with equal speed when the boom broke and cattle once again had not been worth the wear and tear on saddles and ropes to round them up.

Del Rosa had lived as though there would be no tomorrow during the big boom, and when it collapsed had awakened from its binge broke and in debt. The three banks had gone under, foreclosures had wiped out what had been fine ranches, weeds began to grow in branding corrals throughout the range. Even Major Webster Fitzroy, who was said to have once been worth more than a million, had been forced to give up his lavish entertainments and live closer to the hub, although he was still far better off than any other brand owner around.

No trail herd had moved out of the Del Rosa in a dozen years. But Stacy Fitzroy had shouted something about a herd having been sold. Vance could see great activity in Sam Houston Street. The dusty thoroughfare and the sidewalks under the arcades should be deserted, and the stores closed, for this was the *siesta*, when peace reigned. Peace and apathy. It was a custom that had returned after the feverish years of the trail days.

But Del Rosa was now wide awake and churning. Apparently going loco. Men seemed to be doing Highland flings in the street. Women joined them, and they clasped hands, whirling like children in a wild dance. Other men were cavorting and hurling their hats in the air. The sound of excited whooping came to him.

He urged his horse ahead. The pack trail returned to the main stage road where it entered Sam Houston Street from the south. "They're all drunk as owls," he told his horse.

He sighted Stacy Fitzroy. Still sitting on her horse, she was surrounded by yelling, cheering citizens. She was laughing wildly, tipping her hat and gigging her mount with a spur into doing fancy side-stepping.

A rickety ranch wagon came careening along the road, carrying a bug-eyed driver, with a woman and two wide-mouthed children clinging to the seats. Vance pulled his horse aside and let the rig roar past. He recognized them. Olaf Johansen and his family from over on Sawmill Flat.

Olaf had been one of the high flyers when the skyrocket was going up. Afterward he sawed mesquite firewood for sale, chopped cotton and even walked sheep in the Hatch River country in order to furnish food and shelter for his family.

Vance watched the Johansens pile out of the wagon and join the revelers. The elders evidently had already been sampling strong spirits. Olaf leaped in the air, cracked his heels together, then caught up his wife, swinging her until her heavy skirt billowed like a sail.

Others were pouring into town on horseback and in wheeled vehicles. Vance's horse balked at moving nearer the strange antics ahead. He dismounted, tethered it to a mule yard fence and moved in on foot.

He made out a few intelligible words above the uproar. "Hun'dred thousand, give or take a little fer expenses. Thirty-five a head . . . cash money . . . place called Platte City way up no'th. The major sent word. . . ."

It became clear that the citizens of Del Rosa were intoxicated by something apparently far more potent than alcohol. Vance could think of only one item that had such exhilarating power. Money—a commodity that had been mighty scarce in the Del Rosa country for years.

He grasped the arm of a burly cowman who was hurrying to join the festive gathering. "What's this all about?" he asked.

The man halted impatiently. "Where you been, fella?" he demanded. "Ain't you heard that Major Fitzroy has sent word he's sold—"

He paused, peering and Vance saw in him some of the same speculative curiosity he had noted a short time earlier in Stacy Fitzroy's eyes. This rancher's name was Chuck Hazel, and Vance had known him since boyhood, but not favorably. Chuck Hazel had a reputation for bigotry and hard dealing. He now seized a chance to belittle a man he had never dared antagonize in the past.

"Well, look who's here?" he jeered. "You don't mean they really let you out o' the pen? What's the world comin' to?"

"I asked you a question," Vance said. "What was it that Web Fitzroy sent word about?"

"Didn't they give you five years fer stickin' up thet stage?" Hazel demanded. "Don't tell me it's been that long since—"

"I made myself a promise a while ago," Vance said. "It's one you wouldn't want to crowd me into keeping, Hazel."

"You Jardines always was crooked," Hazel said. "Yore paw never earned an honest dollar in—"

Vance hit him then. Chuck Hazel landed flat on his back in the dust. "I just got through telling you I'd made myself a promise," Vance said. "That was it."

He added, "Get up if you want to settle it."

Chuck Hazel appraised Vance's lean height, measuring the cut of his jaw and the chill in his gray eyes. He was remembering the power of the punch that had leveled him. He continued to lie there.

Chuck Hazel's abrupt plunge into the dust had brought a momentary halt to the whooping and cavorting in the street. Everyone was staring.

It was Stacy Fitzroy, still poised on her horse, with her derby hat cocked in her hand, who was first to speak. "Get up, Chuck Hazel!" she commanded. "Get up and beat the tar out of that—that impudent outlaw!"

Vance eyed her. "It was just that sort of talk that earned a sore jaw for Chuck just now," he said.

"I'd *just* like to see *you* try to strike *me!*" Stacy Fitzroy said.

"I wouldn't aim at your jaw," Vance answered. He glared around at the staring citizens. "What brand of forty-rod have you people been drinking?" he demanded. "You all better go home and sober up."

"It ain't anything that'd concern you, Jardine," a man named Bill Summers said. "Not any at all."

"I take it that it isn't a shindig to celebrate my return," Vance commented.

"That's for mighty sure," Bill Summers replied. "I happen to be sheriff of this county now. The citizens elected me to office last fall. 'Tain't within my authority to deny you the right to show your face around here ag'in, but I warn you that even if the governor might have been hoodwinked into turnin' you loose, folks around here ain't forgot that you turned road agent."

"Your speech of welcome warms me," Vance said. "You've been running for office for a good many years, Bill. Now, you've finally made it. I'm afraid Del Rosa County deserves you. If you've got any further honors to shower on me, you'll find me at my place on Rock Creek."

He looked around, adding, "Provided I've still got a place there. I left a house there. It wasn't what you'd call a mansion, but if anything's happened to it I'll inquire around as to who might have been in the vicinity at the time."

He returned to his horse and mounted. The animal, now that the uproar had died, had no objection to ambling through the citizens whose ranks parted to let Vance ride past.

Only Stacy Fitzroy made comment. "Good riddance!" she said.

Vance tipped his hat. "Oh, but you're not rid of me yet, Miss Anastasia," he said. "I aim to stick around for quite a spell. Maybe even the rest of my life."

Back of him, as he rode out of town along the wagon road that curved southward, he heard the revelry and the shouting resume. His arrival had cast only a momentary cloud on Del Rosa's day of joy.

2

Vance rode slowly on his leg-heavy horse, keeping to the wagon road. At Slide Creek he paused for a time, letting his horse nuzzle the cool, running water. He dismounted and moved upstream a few paces, sprawling on his stomach to drink deeply. Except for Rock Creek, on which his own holdings were located, Slide Creek had the best water in the Del Rosa.

There were memories at Slide Creek. Here was where it had happened—the event that had cost him two years of his life. As the water stilled in the margin of the sand-bottomed pool, he had a misty view of his reflection. He heel-squatted, gazing.

His face was very thin and small lines had appeared at the corners of his mouth and eyes. The points of his jawbones stood out. His lips had the tight look of bitter memories and his eyes held a stony flatness that masked all betrayal of inner emotion.

He wondered just how he had looked that day two years in the past when the mail stage had been held up here at the ford. He could not remember. It had been in another life. All he could recall was that he had been young, independent, with no responsibilities, no worries.

He'd managed to buy a run-down small ranch on Rock Creek, including a shack. He had bought a graded bull and a few Hereford heifers, rounded up a few maverick cows in the Big Thicket far to the south, which he'd branded in the 7-11, and was on his way to building up a herd. There had been only a bare living in cattle, but the Del Rosa was mainly open range, with good grazing, and his brand had thrived.

He had hunted and fished when the whim struck him, attended every range dance and chivaree within two days' ride, courted the prettiest girls and enjoyed life to the full. The fact that many of his neighbors had tried to follow the example of Web Fitzroy and treat him as a leper had only amused him. The major had made it plain that the son of the notorious gambler, Silkhat Jack Jardine, was beneath the notice of upstanding citizens.

Vance's answer to the major's ostracism had been to register his brand as the 7-11. That had done nothing to elevate him in the major's esteem. Nor that of the major's daughter, apparently.

He rode the remaining two miles to his ranch. He steeled himself as he approached the last rise. He did not expect to find his house still standing. Deserted structures were always fair game for petty plunderers. Entire buildings, so handy to wagon roads, had been known to vanish overnight.

In his case, having placed so many burrs under the saddles of his neighbors, he anticipated the worst. He was enormously elated, as he emerged into sight of his place, to discover that his fears had been unfounded. The house not only still stood intact, but seemed to be in surprisingly good condition.

He had rebuilt the original shack which had stood beneath two fine cottonwoods. The lower half of the walls, as high as the window sills, was of native stone, the remainder to the roof plates was of matched cedar logs. A shake-roofed gallery shaded the west side.

Two window panes were broken, but someone had placed cardboard over the openings. A few weeds grew against the tool shed. Woodpeckers had drilled its walls. The pole corral beyond the house had the aspect of recent use. Two horses grazed in the fenced pasture beyond the corral. All-in-all, 7-11 had escaped the wrath of his neighbors and of time.

Smoke was lifting from the pipe on the kitchen roof. A man came to the door as he rode up. This individual was bandy-legged and paunchy. His stomach overhung his wide leather belt. His saddle jeans bagged over the tops of dog-eared boots. His homely face, which seemed as wide as its length, was split by a pirate's long-handled graying mustache.

He held in his hand a skillet which contained

a slab of beefsteak, evidently ready to be placed on the stove. He stood, peering from beneath shaggy brows.

"Howdy, Bandy," Vance said, dismounting. "Whose beef are you eating these days? Not mine, of course."

" 'Tain't really you, now is it, boy?" Bandy Plunkett gurgled. "So they got tired o' seein' you around, an' put you out in the cold, cold world. You didn't have to go over the wall, after all."

"Nope," Vance said. "I walked right out the front gate with the blessing of the warden."

"I heerd about it," Bandy said. "It was in the paper. You shore pulled the wool over their eyes with that hero stunt. I been expectin' you to show up most any day for the last two, three weeks. I was beginnin' to think they'd changed their minds an' had took you back."

"They not only let me out, but they gave me ten dollars and a new fifteen-dollar suit of clothes," Vance said.

Bandy eyed him. "Thet don't look like any fifteen-dollar outfit to me," he commented. "Did you steal it somewhere?"

Vance wore a new pair of pin-striped saddle breeches over new, black saddle boots. His shirt was of good white cotton, and he had on a vest of black watered silk, from the breast pocket of which jutted the tips of two Havana cigars.

"In addition to the ten dollars, I'd stored up some money of my own," he explained. "I played a little poker in San'tone and hung around there a couple of weeks, taking advantage of a small run of luck. When I quit I had enough to buy me some clothes, a forty-four dollar horse, some leather to rig it, and still leave me with a stake that ought to keep the wolf from the door for a couple of months at least."

Bandy Plunkett uttered a cackle of laughter. "Yo're jest like yore paw. You look like him too. More'n you did when they tuk you away. What's all them lies I heerd about you an' this hero stuff?"

"It was all a fake," Vance said. "But it worked."

"The way I read it in a San'tone newspaper, a feller got pinned down under a boulder in the rock quarry where you was workin'. You stayed with him, an' got him loose. Trouble was, there was dynamite with fire in the hole, ready to let go. An' it did let go before you could carry the feller into the clear. What was it like?"

"A regular Fourth of July. You ought to have heard it. A real cannon cracker."

"Both you an' the other jigger was in the hospital fer a spell, accordin' to the newspaper," Bandy snorted. "You didn't mention it in any of yore letters, which was few an' far between. You look all right now. How do you feel?"

"Hungry," Vance said, eying the beefsteak.

"Have you got another of those hanging in the cooler? That'd make a set."

"I never had the pleasure o' dinin' on slow elk with a real hero," Bandy said. "Come in. I got another steak jest the size o' this one."

He added, "It's Fitzroy beef. I don't reckon that'll make it stick in yore craw. Don't look fish-eyed at me. I burned the hide. After all, the grief the major caused the Jardines, entitles you to chaw on some of his beef now an' then. The major's not around. He's a thousand miles away, with about three thousand head o' cattle to worry about. He'll never miss one slow-elked steer when he gits home."

Vance entered the kitchen. It needed considerable action with broom and mop. Grease was thick on, and around, the stove. He moved into the room that served as a parlor. It also needed dusting and brooming, and evidently had not been used in a long time. He had made the furniture from native timber, and upholstered it with leather covering he had cured himself. The bedroom, which was comfortably big and contained two bunks, was in good condition.

Bandy was waiting apprehensively in the kitchen, steaks sputtering in the skillet. "If I'd have knowed what day you was comin' home I'd have tidied up a leetle," he said defensively.

"You never was a top hand with a broom," Vance said. "I can see you've hibernated here quite a spell. That grease on the stove is about two years thick, I'd say."

"I didn't figger you'd mind."

"Mind? I'm thankful! I didn't expect to find the house still standing."

"Well, they did have notions in that direction," Bandy said. "They started to try to bust up the place right after you was took away. Rocks through the windows, ridin' by at night an' puttin' bullet holes in the roof. I slung some birdshot in their direction more'n once. Things ain't been quite so bad lately, although somebody busted a couple o' windows about a week ago while I was out ridin' range. I ain't got around to puttin' in new glass."

Vance looked at a shotgun and a rifle that were racked on the kitchen wall. A six-shooter hung in a holster from a peg. Boxes of shells stood on a shelf.

"Looks like you still keep iron handy," he commented.

"The six-gun and the .44-40 belong to you," Bandy said. "The scattergun is mine. There's a lot of human hides, I reckon, in this country from which birdshot from that gun has been picked."

"Any punctures in Fitzroy hides?"

Bandy grunted regretfully. "The major's too high an' mighty, I reckon, to stoop to night ridin'. To give the devil his due, an' allowin' fer his grudge ag'in—"

27

He broke off as though deciding he was saying too much. Vance felt that he had been about to hear the answer to a question that had been deep in his mind nearly all his life. He had always felt that Web Fitzroy's attitude had a deeper basis than mere snobbery. Some of the petty persecutions the major had inflicted on Vance after his father's death seemed to amount to more than the customary antagonism of big ranchers toward lesser outfits.

On more than one occasion the major had ridden unexpectedly into the 7-11 ranch yard, accompanied by half a dozen of his riders and had looked around for evidence of rustled beef. Always without success. Vance had never beefed a Fitzroy steer in his life.

"You're missing the fun in town, Bandy," he said.

"What do you mean—fun?"

"They're dancing in the streets. They act like they've been gargling loco juice. They seem to think they're rich as thieves. They're babbling about a beef herd that sold for a hundred thousand dollars, and cattle selling for thirty-five dollars a head."

Bandy was staring, awe-struck. "My Gawd!" he breathed. "So thet's it!"

"What's it?"

"Solly Barnes rode by here a couple hours ago, screechin' somethin' I couldn't savvy. I figgered he was drunk. Maybe he wasn't. You don't actually suppose—! Oh, my Gawd!"

"Talk man! Can't anybody tell me exactly what this is all about."

Bandy sank down on a bench and fanned himself with his ragged hat. "What if'n the major's really sold the herd?" he said in wonder. "At thirty-five a haid. Holy smoke!"

"Thirty-five a head. Where?"

"Place called Platte City, I reckon," Bandy said. "Thet's somewhere to hell an' gone way up north. Three thousand head of beef. What does that come to?"

"About this hundred thousand dollars everybody's yelling about," Vance said. "I know where Platte City is. I've heard of it, at least. It used to be a shipping point for some of the last drives. It's on the Union Pacific Railroad, up in Colorado, or maybe Wyoming. Are you trying to tell me Major Fitzroy drove three thousand head of stock up there and sold them at a price like that? Why, cattle haven't been worth anything to my knowledge."

"Looks like things might have changed."

"Were they all the major's cattle?"

" 'Course not," Bandy said. "The day's past when even the major could cut that many Box F beef steers. At that he had more'n a thousand head in the drive. He trimmed his brand right down to the last prime steer. The rest came

29

from other outfits in the Del Rosa. About every ranch, big an' small, pooled all the cattle they could find in the brush. They all tuk solemn oath they'd abide by whatever price the major could git up north."

"When did all this happen?"

"Started last winter. The drive pulled out in March as soon as the grass started greenin', with the major as ramrod."

"But there hasn't been a drive that got through in half a dozen years or more, from what I hear," Vance said. "Everything in Kansas is under fence now. It's a jigsaw puzzle trying to find a way, so much so, they gave it up, not to mention there wasn't much of a market if they'd got there."

"The major figured that a trail herd could make it across the high plains in Colorado, far west of the old route."

"That country's too dry," Vance said.

"The major's been keepin' track of things in newspapers an' weather reports. He said there'd been awful heavy snows in the Rockies early in the winter an' that meant cricks an' gullies on the plains thet air dry, except durin' storms, would be carryin' runoff 'til well into the summer. He's a stiff-necked cuss what thinks the sun rises an' sets right in the palm of his hand, but I got to give him credit. He got the drive through, an' from what we heerd the critters were in good shape when they hit the Platte River. Expenses was small, fer the crew was made up of ranchers who had beef in the pool."

"Sounds like luck to me," Vance commented.

"It was a gamblin' chance."

"Gamble? The major? He never risked even a busted collar button on a game of chance."

"No matter what he called it this time, he talked everybody around here into takin' the chance with him. It wasn't only the weather he guessed right. He preached that a big shortage of beef was at hand back east. He'd kept track o' the market ever since Texas had pulled in its horns an' quit. He began proddin' everybody that prices was bound to skyrocket, 'specially if you could get to market first with prime stuff. The others wasn't easy to convince. Money's been so scarce around here for a long time thet cowhides was used in place of cash. Hides was so worthless a man needed a wagonload of 'em to buy enough grub to feed his wife an' kids."

"I doubt if the major had to skin any cattle to buy grub to live on at Oak Hill," Vance commented.

"Maybe not. But even the Fitzroys ain't been livin' as high on the haunch as they would like folks to believe."

"I ran into Stacy Fitzroy on the pack trail a while ago," Vance snorted. "She was as brattish as ever. She was aboard one of those fancy crossbreds and was dressed like she'd just rode out of a castle in England. She didn't look like she had missed any meals lately."

"Maybe so," Bandy said, "but if the major's really sold that drive at thirty-five a head, it won't be healthy for anybody to say much ag'in the Fitzroys in these parts, no matter how stiff a ramrod they've had up their backs."

"Meaning that I better learn to stay in my place."

"You don't seem to savvy what this would mean in the Del Rosa," Bandy said. "It'd put this range back on its feet. There's hardly an outfit, big or small, that didn't have steers in the drive. Cash money would be their salvation. If it hadn't been for the major, there'd have been no cattle drive, no money. He used spurs to goad 'em. They'll appreciate it."

Bandy added, "Maybe you'll appreciate it too."

"Me?"

"Yes, you. You happen to have forty-two head of your 7-11 steers in that drive. At thirty-five a head, minus expenses, that will give you a nice little stake to start grading up your cattle again."

Vance glared so ferociously that Bandy hastily put the table between them. "What did you say?" Vance demanded.

"Well, I done it," Bandy said doggedly. "I was livin' here at your place, eatin' your grub from the cool cellar, an' eatin' some o' yore beef when other steers wasn't handy. An' glad to have a roof over my head. So I rounded up prime steers I could find in the 7-11 iron an' pooled 'em with the others in the drive."

"You had a hell of a nerve. You didn't ask me if you could do a thing like that. You could have written."

"Couldn't see any harm in it, Vance. Yore steers was jest growin' old an' moss-horned, runnin' free on open range. Another year or two an' they'd only have been good for wolf bait or jerky. Anyway, I knew you wouldn't have anythin' to do with throwin' in with a drive where Web Fitzroy was boss."

"And how about Web Fitzroy? Don't tell me he was overjoyed to take Jardine cattle into the herd? Not him!"

"Well, he didn't exactly have a choice," Bandy admitted. "I sorta drifted yore stuff into the herd at night when he wasn't around. It'd been rainin' hard for a week when they was gittin' the bunch together an' all the cattle was so plastered with mud I heerd it was two weeks up the trail before they could begin to really tally brands. From letters some o' the boys sent back to their families, the major was fit to be tied an' branded when he found he had a jag of 7-11 critters along. But he couldn't do anything about it by that time, so yore stuff went right through to Platte City an' sold with the others. At least I hope so."

Vance laughed and slapped Bandy on the back. "It's all too good to be true, of course," he said. "There's been a mistake somewhere."

Yelling riders came racing past on the wagon road, heading in the direction of town. Vance and Bandy ran into the yard. There were three horsemen. Following was an excited woman driving a flatbed wagon to which several children were clinging. The woman was braced on the seat, her sunbonnet flapping on its strings.

"Herd's sold!" one of the men screeched, fanning his horse with his hat. "Solly Barnes rode by, bringin' the word. Thirty-five a haid! We're headin' fer town to git drunk! Saddle up, Bandy!"

They watched the happy contingent vanish down the trail. "It's beginning to look like there might be some truth in this thing," Vance conceded. Then they rushed into the house to rescue the steaks which were beginning to burn.

As they ate, Bandy brought Vance up to date on affairs in the Del Rosa. It was the usual routine accounting. Eb Ryan had been fatally gored by a bull. George Clancy had married one of the Frame sisters over in Round Valley. It was the oldest one George had hooked up with, Susie. One or two familiar names had left the country in hope of finding better times elsewhere. One or two old-timers had passed away. A few babies had been born. There'd been a gunfight between two Cross K riders over a dance hall girl and both cowboys had died. The girl had been ordered out of the country by Sheriff Bill Summers.

Vance finally asked a question that had been uppermost in his mind from the start. "How about Lisa? How's she been getting along?"

There was the slightest hesitation in Bandy's response. "Yore sister's jest fine, I reckon. Jest fine."

"And the kids?"

"Growin' up. I saw 'em only a few days ago walkin' home from school. Chad's stringin' out now. All legs an' arms, like a new colt. He's pushin' eleven years, ain't he? An' Fern's goin' to be as purty as her mother. Even as purty as her grandmother, an' that's sayin' somethin'. Your mother was a stunner, Vance."

"Did you say they were *walking* home from school?"

"I reckon it don't hurt a couple of healthy youngsters to hoof it. 'Tain't everybody kin afford horses to git kids to school the way things have been goin' in this range."

"It's at least five miles from Hat Creek to the schoolhouse," Vance said angrily. "Fern is only eight years old. What's her father doing, that he can't take time to drive them to school?"

Bandy shrugged. "The buggy got busted up some time ago, an' Roy's never been able to git it fixed. He's only got his one saddle horse.

Work ain't been any too easy to find lately. 'Specially ridin' jobs." He paused, then added, "Roy never did hanker to find a job that might dirty his hands. You know that."

Vance finished his meal in silence. Lisa was his only sister. She had married the handsome, debonair Roy Carvell when she was nineteen. She was five years older than Vance. Although she hadn't been much more than a child when their parents had passed away, she had been his adviser and strength through the growing years when they both had learned what it meant to be the offspring of Silkhat Jack Jardine, the gambler.

Wild blood was their heritage, or so Josiah Slocum, the circuit-riding preacher had declared in one of his fire-and-brimstone sermons. The preacher's pronouncement from the pulpit had set them apart from all others in the Del Rosa.

Over the span of years as he was reaching his six feet of rawhide, cat-quick maturity, Vance had fought fistfights with many of those who had taunted him. They held the memories of their defeats at his hands.

He believed it had also been in defiance of them that Lisa had married Roy Carvell. Roy had appeared in Del Rosa as a rodeo rider, and had won day money in such events as the roman riding and trick roping. He never entered the tough bucking contests nor the bulldoggings and the tie-downs. He hung out with the hardcase gambling and drinking fringe that followed the rodeos.

Lisa had been dazzled into a whirlwind elopement. She had never uttered a word of complaint, nor of criticism of Roy, from the day she had made her vows. Vance had respected her attitude, and had never reproached her. However, it was evident from Bandy's reluctance to talk that she was still paying for her mistake.

He sat staring bitterly into his coffee mug. Bandy heeded his mood and let him remain with his thoughts until he had finished the coffee and had carried his plate and utensils to the bench and dumped them in the dishpan.

"I'm goin' to saddle up an' slope into town to find out if all this happiness is real," Bandy said. "I might be a little late gittin' home." He added, "Might be a little drunk too. Either to celebrate, or to drown my sorrow if what we've heard turns out to be a mistake."

Vance nodded. "I'll scrub the dishes. Get along. I'm going to stay sober and get some sleep. I'll ride over to Lisa's tomorrow. She'll be expecting me. I wrote that I'd show up, sooner or later."

3

Long after Bandy had left for town he sat on a bench outside the kitchen door, rolling one cigarette after another, watching a waxing moon flood the brush with silver.

Coming home, he told himself, had been a mistake. Better to have deeded his claim and what water rights he owned over to Bandy. That would be justified. He hadn't thanked Bandy in so many words for guarding his small holdings during his time in prison. Words hadn't been necessary. Bandy Plunkett and Vance's father had fought side-by-side in the Civil War. It was at Chickamauga that Bandy had taken the wounds that had given him his stubby, awkward gait. Vance's father had carried him off the field, with Union shells and Minié balls almost as thick as the flies that had fed on the blood that pooled at their feet. He had saved Bandy's life, but had taken a wound himself that had eventually brought on his own death.

Bandy had always sat as lookout in the gambling houses where Silkhat Jack Jardine played. It was Bandy who had lifted Silkhat Jack Jardine's body from the chair at the poker table that night in Pat McFee's gambling house in

Del Rosa and had carried him into the open air beneath the clear stars.

"Take care of him!" Bandy had implored, lifting his homely, scarred face to those stars. "He's never been well since the day he carried me off the field at Chickamauga. He never dealt a dishonest card in his life. He never welched on a bet nor turned his back on a friend in need. He's the kind all of us ought to be down here."

Vance had been told the story of Bandy's prayer, for he had been only eleven years old at the time and had been at home asleep the night his father had slumped dead upon the poker table where he was playing a winning hand.

Since that night, Bandy had never touched a card in a gambling house. He had confined his activities, when he made his infrequent trips to town, to the bottle.

Bandy had worshipped Vance's mother and had offered the same devotion to Lisa. He had been Vance's guiding hand from boyhood. That was why he had held his two-year vigil at 7-11 to ward off the wrath of grudge-holding neighbors. Vance understood that Bandy had also watched over Lisa as best he could. Bandy still considered himself in debt to the man who had carried him off the battlefield.

Vance found his throat tight as he thought over Bandy's devotion. He believed that he saw clearly now that he should let the past stay buried. His return to the Del Rosa might only add to the burden of Lisa and her children. The prison stigma was on him, and it would only help prove what the preacher had said about the Jardines. They were cursed with wild blood.

He finally went into the house. He had made up his mind to visit Lisa the following day and make sure she and Chad and Fern were all right, then move on. It was a hard decision.

On this night he did not want to be confined by walls. He brought a tarp and bedding from the house, and stretched out beneath the cottonwoods with a rolled-up blanket as a pillow.

He lay content. He had been caged so long it was paradise to sleep beneath the great canopy of stars. There had been times in the past, working roundup, when he had been forced to rough it, he had vowed he'd somehow fix it so that he'd sleep in a bed of down on a silk pillow. Now, it seemed to him, that this was all a man could ask of life.

He slept. He dreamed of Huntsville. Of the nights when the unyielding heat of summer had enveloped him in prickly torment on his pallet. Of the winters, when the northers came, and the cold seemed to seep through the stone walls into a man's bones.

He began dreaming, strangely, of a girl in a derby hat who arched her brows haughtily, and kept striking him with a golden-handled riding crop. She kept telling him he belonged where he had come from. In Hell!

He awakened to the sound of drunken whooping and the pound of galloping hooves. The riders were coming up the wagon trail from town.

As they thundered past the entrance to the short spur road that led to his ranch house, one of them shouted. "Wake him up, boys!"

A six-shooter opened up. Bullets smashed into the walls of the house. A window pane was shattered. "Damned outlaw!" a man yelled. "You ain't wanted hereabouts!"

More slugs slashed at the house. Vance realized his danger and lay flat where he was. Some of the bullets buzzed by, overhead. The gunfire ended. The sound of hoofs faded up the trail. The night was punctured by one more shot as the roisterers receded into the moonlight.

Vance got to his feet. He had heard other epithets they had shouted. "Jailbird! Gambler's whelp!"

He entered the house, lighted the kitchen lamp and surveyed the damage. The heavy walls had absorbed the majority of the bullets. An upper pane in a kitchen window had been pierced. Two plates and a mug on a shelf were shattered. A pan on the stove had been hit and lay on the floor, a hole in its side.

He moved back to the door, gazing in the direction the raiders had gone. "Welcome home!"

he said. "And to blazing hell with all of you. Now, I *am* home to stay."

He discovered that at least two bullets had ripped holes in the mattresses on the two beds. The window in the bedroom was one that had previously been shattered, and covered with cardboard by Bandy. They hadn't been shooting high merely to frighten. For all they knew he and Bandy were lying in the house, dead or wounded.

He lifted the rifle from pegs on the wall, loaded it and loaded the six-shooter. He carried both weapons with him as he moved his bed tarp to better protection back of a woodpile, farther from the house.

He finally slept. Occasionally ranch wagons or riders passed by on the road. Each time he aroused and lay with the rifle in his hands, waiting, ready to shoot back. Although nearly all of the passersby were drunk and noisy and whooping to the world the story of their sudden rise to affluence, they did not attempt to shoot up the house where the son of Silkhat Jack Jardine was ready to meet all challenge. A few of them shouted taunts and insults, but let it go at that.

It was daybreak when Bandy returned. He alighted with all the grace of a sack of grain falling from the saddle and staggered around the ranch yard until Vance caught up with him and steadied him.

"I need 'nother drink," Bandy mumbled. "Jest one li'l drink. I'm real thirsty."

Vance brought a pail of water from the spring and poured some on Bandy's balding head. "There you are," he said. "On the house."

Bandy sputtered and began to sag. "They was all on the house," he mumbled happily. "Free booze, free girls, free everythin'."

"It's the truth, then?" Vance questioned. "They really sold the herd?"

"Thirty-five dollars a head," Bandy said. "A'ter all expenses, they'll split up more'n one hundred thousand dollars."

Vance spread another tarp and laid Bandy out to sleep it off in the shelter of the wood-pile. "Why we siwashin' it out here, boy?" Bandy sighed. "Ain't the house good enough fer us?"

"I'll tell you in the morning," Vance said.

Bandy was already snoring. He unsaddled Bandy's horse, turned it out to feed and water, then cooked breakfast and made coffee. He searched the house and located a jug which contained a few fingers of tequila. It was the hair-raising concoction that was run across the line from Mexico.

While Bandy slept it off he spent the morning inspecting the ranch. His titled land was small, but was flanked by open range that was used by a dozen or more brands of which Major Webster

Fitzroy's Box F iron had been the most numerous in the past.

Vance had taken over the claim on Rock Creek at a county tax auction of delinquent properties. He had paid for it by hard labor. He had hired out at distant roundups, had broken tough, green horses for the Crown outfit a hundred miles east. He had spent ten hours a day, six days a week, on one end of a long ripsaw in the pit at a lumber mill in the Armadillo Hills. He had performed other chores that took endurance— and muscle—and had also taken toll of his belief in the kindness of humanity. His earnings, to say the least, had been modest.

He had avoided one possible source of making money. The poker tables. Not because he did not have the urge. He had discovered long ago that gambling was in his blood. At times it was a fever in him. He also knew he had a natural talent for it. A true skill. He had become aware of this in the harmless penny ante games men played around roundup camp fires and in bunkhouses when the northers blew.

Men he rode with began tossing in their hands and quitting the circle when he tried to join in the play. He would find himself left alone with the poker deck in his hands, but no opponents.

He was the son of Silkhat Jack Jardine, who had died at a poker table. He was the offspring of a professional who must have known all the tricks of the trade. They believed Silkhat Jack had taught those accomplishments to his son.

He had sold off for a few dollars the scrubs, mosshorns and lumpjaws from the thirty-odd head of cattle he had managed to round up bearing the brand that went with the ranch he had acquired. He had managed to accumulate enough money to buy a good Hereford bull and a few young cows. He kept adding to them from time to time. These, along with the few cows he had retained from the original brand, thrived with constant attention.

Some ranchers believed the 7-11 brand thrived too well. The increase in Vance's herd inside of five or six years was far greater in proportion than that of any other brand in the Del Rosa. There was talk that 7-11 cows must always drop twins, or even triplets. Ranchers who were running cattle in the open range began to tell each other it would be better if the Del Rosa was rid of Silkhat Jack Jardine's son.

Major Web Fitzroy was one of those who believed that not all the calves Vance claimed at the branding fires in the spring, when the range rounded up all young stuff for marking, had been dropped by 7-11 cows.

"Strange that Jardine's she-stuff produces nearly one hundred percent every year when the rest of us are lucky to tally half that from our cows," he had said in Pat McFee's gambling house. "I'm finding a lot of my cows dead, with necks broken from being roped and busted, and their calves missing. What do you suppose happens to those calves?"

Web Fitzroy hadn't known that Vance had entered the gambling room at that moment, and was standing inside the door, listening. The spreading silence had warned the major and he had turned. He was a ramrod-straight, aristocratic man, with a gray, clipped mustache and a skin weathered the hue of old parchment. He preferred to wear a tailored plantation-style coat, ruffled shirt and a flat-crowned, wide-brimmed hat when he came to town for social affairs.

Vance had looked around the saloon. It had been Saturday night and the ranchers had come in as usual for conviviality while the women folk shopped. He had pointed to a rancher in jeans and rundown boots whose small outfit, like his own, bordered on range that was used by the big Fitzroy outfit.

"Maybe you could enlighten the major on what happens to his calves, Del," he had said.

Del Gilbert had almost swallowed the cheap stogie he had been smoking. He had been too startled to answer.

Vance had singled out two more ranchers, George Klink and Buck Rockwell. "Or maybe you could help out the major, George," he had said. "Or you, Buck. Maybe you've got an idea as to who kills the major's cows and sleepers their calves in some other brand."

Sleepering was the range term for earmarking motherless calves in the ownership of the mother when the calf was too young to be branded.

The silence had thickened in the place. At least three faces had turned ashen. The men Vance had named were veteran ranchers. Like their neighbors they had seen prosperity and big reverses. No person had ever looked on them as rustlers.

Web Fitzroy was the first to find his voice. "These men are friends of mine!" he had said, and he was also white-lipped. "Are you trying to . . . ?"

"I was asking them a question," Vance said. "Now I'll ask one of you, major. Did you ever happen to notice that every calf I claim for a 7-11 cow these days happens to be bigger, heavier, better than anything you raise at Box F? That's because I pack salt, doctor worms, see that my stuff is moved to better grazing. I spend money building drift fences to keep scrub stock from the brush, such as mavericks from your own herd, off the range so they won't breed with my cows. I don't have to earmark any calf of mine that loses its mother, really. They're easy to identify. And I don't lose many cows—either to coyotes or rustlers."

He waited, but Web Fitzroy had nothing to say. Every man in the place knew Vance had spoken the truth. In their hearts they knew that the real culprits had been named.

The trio Vance had singled out were armed. So was Vance. He had stood waiting, but they had made no move. They probably were recalling that Silkhat Jack Jardine had been known as very fast with a six-shooter. They had seen Vance win prizes in target contests.

Vance had finally turned and walked out of the place amid that dead silence, leaving Web Fitzroy to face neighbors he had believed in and trusted. The major had refused to pursue the matter and had left the gambling house and headed back to his ranch.

However Vance knew he had delivered a mortal blow to that which Web Fitzroy prized above everything in life—his pride and dignity. Whatever dislike he had held of the Jardines in the past had been increased tenfold by the humiliation he had suffered that night.

Vance was remembering that encounter as he rode on his inspection trip. He crossed the creek, noticing that Bandy had kept the wire fence in tight repair along the stretch of stream that had a tendency to turn into a boghole in rainy weather. The irrigation ditch that fed the big flat where Vance raised three good crops of hay a year, was in top condition. That hayfield was a major reason why Vance's cattle thrived.

He rode through scattered live oak. A few young steers wearing the 7-11 brand broke cover. Cows were lying in the shade of the oaks, chewing cuds. He rode farther. What cattle he saw were in top shape. He found few prime steers left in his brand. Bandy had trimmed the herd expertly in contributing to the beef pool.

He rode back to the house lighter in heart. Lighter than that day two years ago when they'd handcuffed him to the seat in the stagecoach that had carried him on the first leg of the trip to Huntsville. He had been given a five-year sentence. Only a few dollars had been taken in the stage holdup, but the prosecutor had told the jury that he was the son of a gambler who had killed two men in disputes over card games. The judge had languidly told the jury to disregard this, but he could not erase from their minds the prejudice their ears had heard.

Bandy was at the spring dousing cold water on his head when Vance returned. "Waugh!" Bandy moaned.

Vance brought out the tequila jug and a tincup. He sloshed a drink into the cup and handed it over. "Hair of the dog," he said.

The fiery liquor hit bottom in Bandy. He shuddered, but decided he might live after all. He looked at the pistol and rifle Vance was carrying, then jerked a thumb toward the bullet-damaged house.

"Seems like you had visitors last night," he said.

"They only left calling cards," Vance said. "They didn't stop."

"Recognize 'em?"

"Didn't have to. They were just neighbors."

Bandy wagged his head. "Neighbors like Del Gilbert, or George Klink an' Buck Rockwell, I reckon. There are others. You know you earned 'em, Vance."

Vance said nothing. Bandy dubiously eyed the rifle and .45. "Could you get yoreself into trouble ridin' around with smoke poles handy?" he asked.

"As a full-fledged citizen I've got the right to carry arms," Vance said. "I've got a full pardon, not just a parole. Pardons wipe the slate clean."

"Yeah, I know. The governor's got a level head on his shoulders. I reckon he figured you got a raw deal. In addition, he knew yore daddy. Governor Dave Andrews was colonel of the regiment in which yore daddy an' me fought at Chickamauga."

"I didn't know that," Vance said, surprised. "Do you suppose that was one of the reasons he pardoned me?"

"Not exactly," Bandy said. "There were other reasons. The main one bein' you had risked yore fool neck draggin' that feller out of the tight he was in when the dynamite let go. It was about like what your daddy did for me at Chickamauga."

Vance walked into the house and pushed fresh wood into the stove. "After dinner I'll ride over to see Lisa and the kids," he said.

"Hang the guns back on the wall," Bandy urged.

Vance shrugged. "Not this time," he said.

Bandy sighed. He stood glumly watching as Vance rode away after the noon meal with the rifle lashed to the saddle.

Vance rode across range, picking his route through the low, brushy hills. He let the horse set its own pace, which was about what a forty-four-dollar horse would feel like after the ride of the previous day. Vance was in no hurry. In fact, he was burdened by a reluctance. Remembering Bandy's hesitance in speaking of Lisa and the children, he was putting off as long as he could what promised to be a disappointment.

Presently, he had a view from a long distance of the Fitzroy ranch. The house, big and rambling, stood among ancient live oaks on a knoll. The Fitzroys had named it Oak Hill. A wide scatter of out-buildings and corrals were set on slopes and flats below.

At midafternoon he came into the stage and freighting trail that led to San Antonio. He followed this as it wound through the draws, hot, dry, and deserted at this hour. It mounted the low divide beyond which lay Hat Creek.

Topping the rise, he pulled up the horse and sat gazing. His destination was in sight. An aching sorrow came to him. Then dull anger formed.

4

The house stood in a clearing near the ford. It had been built originally as a roadhouse and swing station where stage passengers could whet their throats with something stronger than water while the stage team was being changed. The spot was therefore known as Whisky Ford. It had been abandoned years in the past by the stage line in favor of a bypass that offered easier going and cut a mile from the distance farther west, but freighting teams still used the road.

A man and his family had tried to build up a cattle outfit with headquarters at Whisky Ford and the old roadhouse as their home, but had given up when the beef panic came. Roy Carvell had become owner after his marriage to Lisa. Vance doubted that Roy had sound title to the place even to this day. Land was plentiful, cattle worthless and the county had so many properties in tax arrears that it was always easy for a man to move out if his right was questioned. The hills were full of abandoned claims and shacks that could be occupied.

"Soon as I make a stake, I'll build us the biggest, prettiest danged house in the Del Rosa," Roy had told Lisa. "With lace curtains an' stained glass in the front door. No use wastin' good money on this place. We'll only be here a few months."

That had been twelve years ago. Chad and Fern had been born in this weather-beaten, sagging house. A room had been added to the original rock-and-log-built structure. Its walls were a crazy quilt of scrap lumber, packing case lids, mud-chinked rocks and galvanized sheetiron— whatever material Roy could lay his hands on with a minimum of effort.

In the two years since Vance had seen Whisky Ford Ranch, it had deteriorated sadly. The sheetiron was red-ribbed with rust. The tarpaper on the roof was cracked and had been crudely patched.

The barn, a huge ramshackle structure, which had once served as shelter for the swing teams of the stage line, was a ghostly, weather-blackened pile with holes in the crooked shake roof. The ancient pole corral beyond the barn was in sagging disrepair.

A washing flapped on a clothesline at the rear of the house. A woman wearing a sunbonnet and a gingham apron came from the kitchen carrying a clothes basket and began taking down the garments.

Lisa. Vance's eyes blurred. His sister had sat through the hours of his trial in the Del Rosa courtroom, side-by-side with him, challenging public derision. She had written to him regularly during the two years he had spent in Huntsville, and had come to visit him on the rare occasions when she could find the money for stage fare. It was Lisa's loyalty, above all, that had helped him endure the iron bars and stone walls.

She stood for a moment gazing toward the towering bulk of the barn. She took a step in that direction, then seemed to decide against it, and returned to the kitchen, carrying the basket. At that distance Vance tried to assure himself she had not changed. She still carried herself tall and proud.

Shadows moved within the deeper blue shadows of the barn's open wagon tunnel. Vance made out the shape of a saddled horse that was tethered there.

Not caring for the presence of a stranger, or even of Roy at this meeting with his sister, he circled the clearing, reaching the creek and approached the house so that its bulk hid his arrival from whoever was in the barn.

Lisa came to the kitchen door when she heard him ride up. She came with a rush to meet him. She kissed him, held him very tight for a long time, not daring to speak.

"I've expected you every day, brother," she choked. "Ever since you wrote that you were free."

"I told you it might be a couple of weeks or more," Vance said.

"I know," she said, and tried to smile. She held him at arms' length. "You've changed."

"For the better, I hope." He tried to say it lightly. He tried to grin. Lisa had changed also. Careworn lines had deepened. He fancied he saw the first hint of gray in her hair that had once been a golden chestnut hue, but now seemed tarnished. Her calico waist and skirt were scrupulously clean, but threadbare. She had wrapped her hands in the folds of the apron and he knew it was to hide from him the marks of toil and their thinness.

But her indomitable spirit was still there. She kept trying to smile joyously. She must have sensed that within him was a growing rage that he tried to hide from her.

"The kids?" he inquired. "Bandy tells me they're growing up. They're in school, of course?"

"Yes," she said. "It will be an hour or so before they get home."

She led him into the kitchen. There was tension in her. He put it down to reluctance to display their poverty. The interior had deteriorated also during the two years. It, too, was meticulously clean, but the gingham curtains were frayed and tattered. Holes that time and heat had worn in the stovepipe had been rudely covered by flattened tin cans, held by pieces of baling wire. The stove itself, which had been an ancient relic when Lisa had come here as a bride, looked like it might fall apart any day. A broken leg on the table had been replaced by a two-by-four, held by nails. Chairs were in the same sorry state of makeshift repair.

The living room was no better, although Lisa had contrived to hide some of the work of time on furniture and carpet with needlework and rag rugs.

"I'll fix a bite to eat," she said. "And coffee."

She rushed back to the kitchen—to hide her emotion and shame. He placed his hat on the antler rack alongside the door and followed her into the kitchen.

"Where's Roy?" he asked.

"Around somewhere," she said, keeping her face averted. "I'll call him."

"Never mind," Vance said. "He'll be along. I saw a saddled horse in the barn. Visitor?"

"Oh, yes," Lisa answered. "I'd forgotten. It's one of the neighbors who happened to drop by. He and Roy are out there yarning, I guess. Roy probably doesn't know you are here."

But he knew she hadn't forgotten about the visitor in the barn. Lisa had never been good at evasion.

"Never mind about anything to eat," he said. "Coffee will do right now."

He filled the cups Lisa sat on the table. The cups were chipped and one was cracked. They were from the set of fine ware he had given Lisa and Roy as a wedding present.

"Did you hear about the big celebration in town?" he asked.

Lisa hadn't heard. He told her what he knew about the sensational news that Web Fitzroy was returning from the north with what amounted to a fortune.

"Now isn't that just wonderful!" Lisa cried. "I'm so glad. Times have been so hard. So very, very hard. For everyone. I'm so glad for all of them."

He rolled a cigarette and lighted it. He had his answer to the question he didn't want to ask. Lisa was glad for them. For the others. It was plain she would not benefit from the windfall. Roy had no cattle in the pool.

A shadow had dampened her animation. She moved around the kitchen. She tried to talk lightly, chattering about the children, about mutual acquaintances, about the weather.

About everything except herself and Roy. And about the visitor who stayed out of sight in the barn. She glanced from the window occasionally. Presently he heard a rider leaving. He arose and moved toward the window. Lisa tried to divert his attention by hurriedly bringing up some new story about the children. She even moved into his path.

Over her shoulder he saw the man who rode

away. He stood, cup in hand, watching the visitor ride into the brush down the creek. He was a roughly dressed individual with a hard, square-jawed face.

Vance knew Lisa was watching him. There was apprehension deep in her eyes. The fury again built up in him. "I see that Len Kelso is still around," he said, trying to be casual.

"Yes," Lisa answered. "Len still has his place at Dry Fork. I guess Roy has a jug in the barn and they were having a drink together."

She seemed to feel she needed to add something. "After all, it's no crime to offer a neighbor a drink, is it?"

"In this case I wouldn't know," Vance said. "I never had a drink with Len Kelso."

He poured more coffee. From the window he saw Roy Carvell heading on foot toward the house. Roy was still handsome, but his features had hardened. He had always dressed nattily. In contrast to Lisa's much-mended garb, his shirt was new and of the double-breasted pattern. His dark trousers were bagged over the tops of his boots with studied effect. A pearl-gray hat hung on the back of his yellow hair.

Vance set the cup down, left the kitchen and walked to meet his brother-in-law. He didn't want Lisa to hear what he had to say to Roy. He guessed that she knew this, for she made no attempt to follow him.

Roy halted in mid-stride when he saw Vance. He gave the impression he was wildly excited about something—and a little frightened. That changed to a defensive frown as he recognized Vance. He erased that swiftly and came rushing forward, a hand outstretched.

"Vance, old boy!" he exclaimed. "I'm glad to see you! You're lookin' mighty well!"

Vance avoided the handshake. Instead, he grasped Roy by the arm, whirled him and walked him back to the barn and into its dimness out of Lisa's sight.

He grasped Roy by the front of his shirt, shaking him. "You whelp!" he said between set teeth.

Carvell was ashen. "My God, Vance! What's wrong? What've I done?"

Vance drew back a knotted fist. He restrained himself in time. "You gave your word you'd take better care of Lisa and the kids," he rasped. "You made a promise to me. You haven't changed, have you? She goes around in rags while you play the dude. Look at that house she lives in! Look at this place! Is this what you said you'd do when I was fool enough to spend years of my life so Lisa and the kids wouldn't be disgraced?"

Roy tried to bristle with anger and injured dignity. "I done all a man could!" he protested. "Times has been real hard around here, Vance. 'Tain't been easy to—"

Vance hit him. He drove the blow to the

stomach, for he didn't want to put a mark on Roy that Lisa could see. "You whimpering, stuffed leppie. To think I was stupid enough to believe you'd ever change."

The punch bent Roy double. He gasped for breath, clutching his stomach. "Don't hit me ag'in," he pleaded. "Damn you, Vance, you ain't human. You never did like me. I never asked you to go to the pen fer me."

"I didn't do it for you," Vance said. "I did it for Lisa and the kids. I wouldn't wipe my boots on you. You promised me you'd earn an honest living at least."

"That's what I've tried to do," Roy blustered.

"By still hanging out with Len Kelso? Everybody knows he's bad medicine. He left you to hang and rattle once, and I paid for it. Won't you ever learn?"

He gave Roy a contemptuous shove, sending him sprawling on the dusty barn floor. He turned to leave, fearing that if he stayed he might vent on Roy all the pent-up bitterness and frustration of those years in Huntsville.

He found himself staring into the startled eyes of Stacy Fitzroy. She was on foot, holding the reins of a saddlehorse. The soft loam that had accumulated over the years around the barn had muffled the arrival of a rider. She evidently had dismounted and had been leading the animal toward the shade of the structure.

"Oh!" she exclaimed, confused. Her eyes swung to Roy Carvell, who was staggering to his feet, still nursing his stomach. "I'm—I'm sorry!" she stammered. "I only meant to leave my horse here to cool."

She added, as though Vance had demanded something. "I—I just got here!"

Her confusion passed. Stacy Fitzroy had never been one to be at loss for long in the presence of others, particularly a Jardine. Still leading the horse, she turned and walked toward the house. She was not the fashionable figure of the previous day. Her horse was rigged with a stock saddle and she wore a divided skirt and cowboots, both of which had seen much service. A neckerchief was knotted around her throat and a calfskin vest protected her cotton blouse. A hat hung on her back, held by the chinstrap.

She had pointedly ignored Roy Carvell and had asked no questions. Vance watched her approach the house and free a bundle, wrapped in brown store paper that had been lashed to the cantle.

He wondered just how long she had been standing in the entrance to the barn, and how much she had heard. He turned on Roy. "Get yourself a job. An honest job. See to it that Lisa has it easier. Decent clothes to wear, a decent house to live in. Stay away from Len Kelso. He'll be hung for rustling, sooner or later, if not for something worse."

Roy tried to salvage some of his pride. "You ought to be mighty glad I ain't packin' my gun right now, Vance, or I'd ask you to draw. I swear, if'n you ever put a foot on my place ag'in I'll put a slug in you."

"I'll be back," Vance said. "And if things don't change for the better for Lisa and the kids real quick, what I did to you just now is only a puny start."

Lisa had come to the door of the house and had ushered in Stacy Fitzroy, carrying the bundle. "What's Stacy Fitzroy doing here?" Vance asked.

"How would I know?" Roy replied sullenly. He added apprehensively, "Do you reckon she came snoopin' around here in time to hear anything she wasn't supposed to?"

"That," Vance said, "is something for you to fret about."

"Hell, it wouldn't make no nevermind to her which one of us it was," Roy said, gaining confidence. "Them Fitzroys never had any use fer you Jardines. I'm goin' to tell Lisa to run her off if she tries to come around here ag'in."

A suspicion that had been lurking in Vance's mind came to a stabbing point. "She's been here before?" he demanded. "Why?"

"I reckon she likes to pass the time o' day with Lisa," Roy said hastily. "After all, women like to git together an' talk. Even Stacy Fitzroy."

"But not with a Jardine," Vance snapped. "Not

unless it makes her feel high and mighty over us. If this is what I'm thinking it might be . . ."

He strode to the house. The front door through which Stacy Fitzroy had entered, still stood open. He almost collided with her as he stalked into the parlor. She apparently had been about to leave. The paper-wrapped bundle lay on the sofa.

"Just a minute!" Vance said. He pointed to the bundle. "What's that?"

"None of your double-blasted business," Stacy Fitzroy said. "And take off your hat when you're in the presence of ladies."

Vance removed his hat with an elaborate flourish and addressed his sister. "Excuse me, Lisa," he said.

Lisa was crimson with humiliation. "Please, Vance! Don't be rude."

Vance picked up the bundle, broke the string with which it was tied. The brown paper unfurled and a shower of garments spilled upon the sofa—dresses and undergarments for a child about Fern's age—breeches, shirts, shoes and stockings that would fit Chad.

All the items were new, bearing the creases of storage on shelves. Vance guessed they had been bought very recently in Del Rosa.

"So that's it!" he said. If Lisa was crimson with shame, his humiliation was of a different nature. He was ashen. He gathered the garments and furiously wrapped the paper around them and tied the bundle with the string.

"We don't want nor need your charity," he said.

He tried to jam the bundle into Stacy Fitzroy's arms. She refused to accept it. "I don't see where you've got any right to have anything to say about it!" she blazed.

Vance hurled the bundle at her feet. "Carry it back to where you got it! The Jardines take care of their own."

Stacy Fitzroy's voice was shaky. "By being sent to prison? By—by being so—so hard? So tough?"

Vance picked up the bundle, walked outside and tied it on the saddle of Stacy Fitzroy's horse. She followed him. She was pale, but if she was frightened of him she refused to quail.

She spoke to Lisa. "It wasn't charity. You know that, Lisa. It was a birthday gift to the children. From me. Because they're so nice, so cute. Because they're children. Because they deserve to be—to be—" She didn't finish it.

Vance did it for her. "Because they deserve to be dressed as well as the other children. They will be. We'll see to that. But it won't be paid for by a Fitzroy."

"I'm sorry, Lisa," Stacy Fitzroy said. "I spoke to your husband a few days ago, asking if I might give Fern and Chad something for their birthday.

Both of their birthdays come up this week, I know. He said it would be all right."

She moved to the horse, to mount. "Why be so infernally proud?" she said to Vance.

"That's odd advice, coming from a Fitzroy," he said.

She studied him with eyes dark and brooding. Eyes that did not hold their customary disdain of him. He felt that she was assessing him from a new viewpoint. Then she swung into the saddle and rode away without looking back.

Vance looked at his sister. "Don't tell me you meant to accept that stuff?"

She did not speak. Her silence was the answer.

"From a Fitzroy?" He was horrified.

When Lisa still did not respond, he walked to his horse and headed away from Hat Creek.

5

Instead of returning to his place on Rock Creek, Vance changed his mind and followed the stage trail into Del Rosa. Anger toward his brother-in-law still smoldered. He held the pace down, for the district schoolhouse that served ranch children in this section lay ahead.

It was late afternoon and classes were over for the day. He began meeting pupils who were homeward bound. Only a few who had short distances to go were on foot. The others were mounted double, or even triple on gentle horses, or had been picked up by housewives driving ranch wagons. Older boys were arrogant on young horses that were wild-eyed and kicking up dust.

Long after the last straggler had passed, he came upon two small figures on foot, carrying lunch pails. They were barefoot and deeply tanned. Hatless, Fern's hair was burnished by the sun to a golden hue. Chad, who had also inherited Lisa's fine gray eyes and features, was lank and solemn.

At first they shied away from him when he halted his horse. Fern was a slender child, with the promise of great beauty. She wore calico that, like her mother's, was scrupulously cared for, but patched and threadbare. Chad's corduroy pants and shirt were faded and worn.

"I'm your Uncle Vance," he said. "I was over to your place to visit your mother and rode this way to meet you."

They both still stood stiff and aloof. But they had been taught their manners. "I hope you are well," Chad said politely.

He and Fern were a little frightened, but not wanting to show it. Vance found a chill working inside him. He had seen this look in adults also. It was the expression that came when they knew they were gazing at a man who had been convicted as a road agent. An outlaw.

Vance wanted to take them in his arms. They were of his own flesh and blood. Neither they nor Lisa knew he had taken the blame for a robbery their father had committed. Gazing now at their troubled young faces, he realized they had not entirely escaped the stigma. Their schoolmates, no doubt, had seen to that.

In addition, they were of Jardine blood. Wild blood. Their grandfather had been a gambler, and had killed two men. The fact that he had drawn both times in self defense against ruffians who had tried to rob him, was beside the point. Their mother had eloped with a ne'er-do-well and they lived in poverty at Whisky Ford, a place that had a notorious past.

Vance alighted from the horse. "Shake," he said to Chad.

The boy extended a tentative hand and Vance gripped it. "I'm home to stay, Chad," he said. "I intend to build up the brand, and maybe you will want to help me. We Jardines will stick together from here on in. And we'll spit in the eye of anybody who looks crossways at us."

He touched Fern's hair, and said, "You are a very pretty girl. I'm proud to be your uncle."

He mounted, and added, "I'll see you again tomorrow."

As he rode on toward town, the memories of the past were as vivid as if it had happened yesterday. The holdup had been staged by a lone masked man, and it had been a blunder from start to finish. There had been no treasure box aboard the coach when it was stopped at dusk at the Slide Creek ford. In fact, there had been less than thirty dollars, all told, in the pockets of the three passengers who had been aboard.

To make matters worse, as far as the road agent was concerned, Major Webster Fitzroy and three other ranchmen, bound toward Del Rosa, had come upon the scene and had opened fire. However the masked man had escaped on his horse into the brush. Darkness had fallen so that it was daybreak before his trail was picked up by Juan Sonora.

The trail led to Vance's 7-11 ranch on Rock

Creek. The man who fled from the house at the approach of the trailers in a futile attempt to escape on foot into the brush turned out to be Vance. They found in his pockets the money that had been taken from the stage passengers, along with a gold watch and a ring that had been seized from one of the fares. They found the horse the masked man had been riding, with a bullet burn in its haunch. They found in Vance's house a black silk scarf of the kind the road agent had used for a mask.

What they did not find was Roy Carvell, hidden in the brush along the creek where he had taken refuge. Vance had kept a tight lip during the trial that was held later in the little courtroom in Del Rosa. The trial lasted only an hour, and the jury returned the guilty verdict within minutes.

Vance had felt that he owed it to Lisa for the sacrifices she had made in being almost a second mother to him. He felt also that he had been repaid because it had spared Chad and little Fern the full blow.

He had hoped it would be a lesson to Roy. Apparently that hope was in vain. It was Len Kelso who had planned the holdup for which Vance had taken the blame. Roy Carvell and Kelso had been drinking and poker-playing partners. There were rumors that Kelso had been in bad trouble up north and had fled to Texas. He was suspected of petty rustling and of running wet horses in from Mexico during the five or six years he had been in the Del Rosa, but he had managed to stay out of serious trouble with the law.

Vance had forced the truth of the holdup out of Roy the night his brother-in-law had come to his ranch on a spent horse. Roy had been in terror, believing pursuit was close on his heels. Len Kelso had told him there would be treasure on the stage. The plan was for Kelso to be aboard as a passenger who would take a hand in case there was resistance. Kelso, however, had not been on the stage. Roy, later, had told Vance that Kelso had learned there would be no treasure aboard, but he had said he was unable to get word to Roy in time to avoid the holdup.

At least that was Kelso's story. Vance believed the truth was that Kelso, after talking Roy into holding up the stage, had no intention of being aboard, but planned on sharing in the profits if Roy really had been successful in getting away with treasure. As it turned out, Vance was the one who had paid the penalty.

Darkness had come by the time Vance arrived in Del Rosa, but the town was ablaze with lights and swarming with activity. There was music, singing and whooping, punctuated often by blasts from six-shooters being fired into the air.

An uproarious square dance was in progress in the principal block in Sam Houston Street, from which all vehicles and horses had been barred. Women swung the hems of their skirts and men bowed and scraped. A brass band blared. Alamo Street, where the music halls and gambling houses were located, rocked to the beat of drums and banjos.

Del Rosa was celebrating its good fortune. Evidently the word had gone far, for Vance saw ranchers present from the Bucksaw Hills a hundred miles away. He had to tether his horse beyond the fringe of town, for there was no room closer.

He moved down Sam Houston Street, shouldering his way among the revelers. "Looks like everybody's ready to live mighty high, friend," he observed to a cowman who was drunk and happy.

"This here is only the slow start, mister," the man, who was a stranger to Vance, chortled. "Wait'll we git our hands on thet beef money. Then we'll pick up this here town, give her a spin an' watch her fly."

"When will that be?"

"Tomorrow," the man whooped, and leaped, kicking his heels together.

"Tomorrow? I thought the major and the rest of them were on their way from this Platte City. That's a long piece from here."

"Thet's whar the major played it real slick," the man explained. "Him an' some of the other boys come home by train as fur as San'tone. They hired a special stagecoach to fetch 'em the rest o' the way. They pulled into the Fitzroy spread at Oak Hill a day or two ago. Then the major sent word as to what he'd done. He had kept it a secret 'til he got home safe with the money. Sugar brings flies, you know."

"He's at Oak Hill with the money?" Vance questioned. "But why didn't he bring it on into town?"

"The mayor asked him to hold off 'til we could arrange to welcome him an' the other boys in style, which will be tomorrow. There'll be the dangedest parade an' hoe-down you ever seen. Speeches, fireworks an' all the trimmin's. They're startin' already to roast four fat oxen. The major will divvy up the money with such brand owners as had beef in the pool drive. I had two hundred head in the herd. We'll go on the biggest bender in the history o' Texas, an' thet means the whole blasted world."

"I'd say everybody's off to a running start," Vance grinned.

Pop Rogers's store was still open. Pop sold everything from horseshoes to ladies' millinery, from baby powder to gunpowder. As Vance entered the door he came face-to-face for the second time that day with Stacy Fitzroy.

Both halted, glaring, waiting for the other to make a move. Then she brushed past him and was lost among the cross tides of humanity on the street.

There were only one or two other shoppers in the big, cluttered room. Pop Rogers, in person, came to face him across the counter after he had stood there for several minutes, waiting.

"Whatcha want?" Pop demanded. His manner was not cordial. He was a gangling, graying old-timer with a moth-eaten mustache. Some said he'd been in the Del Rosa since the sun was no bigger than an orange. Others said that was stretching it a bit. One thing was certain. He had to wear a skull cap to cover the loss of a considerable patch of hair. That proved he had been around when the Comanches were raiding down from the Staked Plains. A Comanche had tried to lift his scalp with a war ax.

It was also said Pop had the first penny he had taken in, as well as its successors. He had never been one to appreciate the viewpoint nor the personality of a chance-taking, colorful person, such as Silkhat Jack Jardine. Nor that of Jack Jardine's son.

"Howdy, Mr. Rogers," Vance said, knowing he had always been a thorn in Pop's side.

"What d'yu want?" the lank man repeated testily.

"I'm in the market for clothes that would please a boy who'll be eleven years old in a few days and a nice little girl of eight," Vance said.

"My nephew and niece, Chad and Fern Carvell."

The storekeeper seemed to be startled. He glanced toward the door through which Stacy Fitzroy had gone, as though he had a sudden disturbing thought.

"Clothes?" he stammered.

"Sure," Vance said. "Chad looked pretty big for his age. He must be growing fast. Fern too. So pick sizes that won't get too small for 'em in a hurry. Shirts, pants for the boy, dresses and underwear for the girl. Shoes, stockings, too. Shoes, above all. The best you've got in stock."

Pop glared at him. "My policy's cash," he said. "Cash on the barrelhead."

"A smart policy," Vance agreed.

"What you're askin' fer will run up to a snug amount. Twenty dollars or more, I'd say at a guess."

"More than that before I get through, most likely," Vance said. "I don't want any shoddy stuff. No linsey-woolsey, no butternut. Good, first-class cotton and wool. Good shoe leather. And I want the prettiest doll you got in the place for Fern. And a rabbit gun for Chad. That .22 there on the rack might do. The one with the fancy carving on the stock."

"Thet gun's worth twelve-fifty alone," Pop snorted.

"Do you want to sell me the stuff I'm asking

for, or do I have to get me a Sears Roebuck catalogue and write out an order?"

"Where would *you* git the money to pay fer it?"

Vance gave him a long, silent look. Pop backed off a step. "All right, all right!" the man mumbled. "But you better not try no flim-flam on me, you hear me?"

He began shuffling up and down the shelves, picking out items and tossing them on the counter. Vance inspected each purchase closely. He recognized a blue dress about Fern's size and a pair of boy's corduroy breeches. They were the same garments that had spilled from the bundle Stacy Fitzroy had brought to his sister's house.

He realized that accounted for her presence in the store. Evidently she had returned the purchases and was leaving as he arrived.

He started to scornfully toss these garments aside. He wasn't going to let Pop Rogers get away with palming off on him any items that Stacy Fitzroy had selected.

Common sense prevailed. It occurred to him that Stacy Fitzroy, being a woman, was, beyond question, better qualified to judge just what was needed in a matter of this kind. He had to grudgingly admit that, as far as he could see, she hadn't stinted on cost in buying these gifts for Chad and Fern.

"Best quality in the store," Pop snapped,

resenting the way Vance kept pawing through the growing stack of items, seeking something to complain about. "Better'n you'd git out'n a mail order catalogue. Better'n you'd find in any store, even in San'tone, if you ask me."

"Wait until I ask you," Vance said.

Pop lifted the new .22 out of the case and laid it alongside the wearing attire. Vance pointed out a flaxen-haired doll with a fluffy dress that was the best of a meager assortment in the toy case. "That one," he said.

"Thet doll brings a dollar an' a quarter!" Pop warned him.

"Looks like it might be almost worth it," Vance said. "Tote up the bill."

He drew from his pocket a roll of greenbacks, held by a rubber band. The storekeeper's eyes bugged, and he had to start totaling the bill all over again. He couldn't help making another verbal mistake. "Now where'd a man jest out o' the pen git a roll of—?"

He ended it with a frightened gurgle. The look in Vance's eyes was like a steel spike, impaling him.

"You were saying . . . ?" Vance asked silkily.

Pop, his gnarled fingers quivering, concentrated on adding up the bill. "Forty-seven dollars an' eighty-seven cents," he said, swallowing hard.

"Add two bits worth of gumdrops and as many

chocolate drops," Vance said. "And two boxes of .22s. Longs and shorts."

He counted out fifty dollars in greenbacks and watched Pop examine them suspiciously with the air of a man expecting the bills to turn out to be counterfeit. Disappointed, the storekeeper grudgingly counted out the change.

"Wrap it up and keep it here until I call for it, or send someone for it," Vance said. "That'll be tomorrow most likely."

"Now I ain't goin' to be responsible for—"

"But you are," Vance said. He watched until the wrapping was finished, tied the bundle himself with string from Pop's spindle, then left the store.

He believed he knew where he would find one friend, at least, in Del Rosa. He made his way through the throng on Sam Houston Street, pausing for a time to watch the dancing. He kept time to the music with a foot, finding pleasure in the animation of the women and the high-flying of the men.

The name of Major Webster Fitzroy was on every lip, almost with reverence. He was the savior of the Del Rosa. He had gone like a knight in armor, leading a lost cause, and was returning with the Holy Grail. He had led them out of the wilderness of poverty and despair, put them back on their financial feet, made free men and women of them.

It had not always been this way. In the past Web Fitzroy's poker-backed aloofness had rankled with his neighbors. They had their own pride, and it had never set well with them to be looked down on as inferiors by the owner of the biggest outfit in the range who worshipped tradition and family lineage.

All that seemed forgotten now. "Here's to Major Fitzroy!" a drunken man kept shouting. That was the toast of the day—or rather of the night—and it was being drunk repeatedly and heartily.

There were only a few malcontents who stood on the sidelines, hands in pockets, envious, perhaps, because they had refused to trust their cattle to the major's care.

"There'll be no livin' with Web Fitzroy after this," Vance heard one sour-faced cattleman say to a companion. "We'll all be dirt under his boots, fer sure, now thet he's managed to sell the herd."

"I got to admit he's got cause to ride high in the stirrups," the other man said.

"The major won't be bashful about takin' all the credit," the first man grunted. " 'Twon't be long before he'll be lettin' people think he kin walk on water. He—"

The man broke off. He had been suddenly confronted by Stacy Fitzroy, who had been moving through the crowd, and had halted when she overheard some of the remarks.

79

She stood glaring. Vance expected violence. In the past he had seen demonstrations of her capacity for making the fur fly. That had been in their school days when events had not gone exactly according to her wishes. In fact Vance had been the one who had usually laid the powder train that had touched off the explosions. And had applied the spark.

The two men evidently expected to be struck by no less than lightning. They stood rooted, withering under her scorching gaze. Vance told himself it was fortunate she did not have a gun handy—or even her riding crop.

She turned suddenly and walked away. She hadn't known Vance was present, and came face-to-face with him once more. He saw torment in her eyes, and tears of anger.

"Damn them!" she sobbed. "Damn all of you! Can't I go anywhere without finding you leering at me?"

She fled into the crowd. She still wore the rough riding garb. She was still sobbing.

6

Vance walked to Alamo Street and entered the music hall and gambling house named the Blue Star. Except for Pop Rogers's general store, it was housed in the biggest building in town. Plank-built, hip-roofed, it had the crazy angles of a structure that had seen many alterations and additions. The Blue Star had seen its boom days when famous entertainers had appeared on its stage in the dance hall. It had seen its bad times when only the saloon had operated.

Tonight, the Blue Star had turned back time to the days of its glory. The dance hall blazed with light and was fogged with tobacco smoke and the dust that was being kicked up by dancing men and women. Staid ranch ladies, who had always lifted their noses at the mention of the Blue Star's wild old days, were now fulfilling their secret ambition, to dance in the music hall where spangled garters and scanty skirts had been the order of the night in time gone by.

The Blue Star was owned by Pat McFee, who had been Silkhat Jack Jardine's friend. He had also been Vance's friend. Vance wondered if Pat would still be a friend as he moved toward the long room which was given over to the gambling tables.

Two faro layouts were in operation, along with roulette and birdcage tables and dice throws. The main attraction were the poker tables, of which five were in action.

Every table was feverishly busy. Vance could not recall ever seeing so many men who appeared obsessed with the urge to try their luck. He knew many of the players. The majority were ranchers who had been grubbing for a living in the hills for years. Normally they were sober-minded men with wives and children to think about. Vance doubted if many of them had ever risked more than a dollar on a gambling game in the past. Now they were riding high.

He saw that very little actual money was being used. IOUs, scrawled on squares of paper that stood handy on the tables, were the main medium of currency. A scattering of cash was in sight, greenbacks, silver coins and a few goldpieces, but this was minor in comparison to the sums represented by the slips of paper that were changing hands at every table.

Pat McFee sat in the dealer's chair at the biggest poker table, which had five chairs in place. Only stud poker was played at this table, and it was in operation only when Pat McFee took over the dealer's chair.

The other poker tables were for open play, with the rules set by the house, one of which was that a percentage of every pot would go to the house when the bell in the clock on the wall struck the quarter hour.

Contrary to tradition, the stakes at the stud table seemed to be the smallest in the room. The play there lacked the hectic pace of the other games. This, Vance saw, was because only cash was being used. There were no IOUs at the stud table. This had always been Pat McFee's rule.

"A man loses only what money he brings into the game when I am dealing," Pat McFee had said.

A hand of stud had just been finished, the pot raked in by the winner. Pat McFee looked up and saw Vance. He was a blocky-shouldered Irishman with a face that bore the marks of roughhouse battles in the past. Vance could not recall ever seeing Pat without the brown derby hat that was tilted forward to shade his eyes as he played. It was said Pat wore the hat even to bed. The fact was that Pat was a vain man who possessed only a fringe of ginger-colored hair around a pate as glistening as a cue ball.

Pat sprang to his feet, a wide grin creasing his homely features. " 'Tis you, me boy!" he shouted, and kicked back his chair, offering a hand.

He made a display of it, standing there pumping Vance's hand. He wanted them all to know he was not turning his back on the son of his old friend. It had been at the stud table that

83

Vance's father had died. No other person than Silkhat Jack Jardine and Pat McFee had ever dealt at that table. Since the death of his old friend only Pat McFee had occupied that chair.

Vance once again felt his throat tighten. He could hardly have blamed Pat if it had been the other way. Play paused at the other tables as men looked at this scene and understood what it meant. The ripple of attention spread to the bar and to the dance floor. Men, glasses in their hands, came to peer. All Del Rosa was being told that Vance Jardine was home and had at least one friend left. That friend was Pat McFee, gambler and owner of a music hall.

"Sure an' it's a sight for old eyes," Pat said. "I hear you are a hero, Vance, me lad. Saved a man's life, an' almost went through the Pearly Gates yourself, so the newspapers in San'tone said. For that I will buy you a drink."

"Thanks," Vance said, knowing that Pat never drank during business hours. "I'm riding high enough. I don't need another lift. Thanks for everything."

"What can I do for you, lad?" Pat asked.

"You've done enough already," Vance said. "I've got a few dollars I've got the urge to try to run up to about the size of a pony, or maybe a good, slow mare."

"Pony?" Then Pat understood. "For Lisa's two buttons?"

Vance nodded. "Their birthdays are coming up."

"Sure an' that would be a fine present, me lad. I would be happy to loan you the money."

"Thanks again," Vance said. "But I prefer to try my luck."

"It does not always smile even on worthy causes," Pat warned. "What do you wish to play?"

Vance surveyed the crowded room. "Poker, of course," he said.

Pat pointed to the chair he had been occupying. "There it is, me boy."

"Your place, Pat? Now, I can't—"

"For tonight," Pat said. He leaned close and whispered, "Bad cess to a lazy husband that neglects a fine wife an' two young ones. Take my place. It is your right. Your father sat there. I have tried to help Lisa. She would have none of it. I could only try to send money on the sly. She always knew from where it came and sent it back. She will have none of gambling or gamblers. Never let her know you have touched a poker deck. She can never forget that your father died at this poker table."

Vance hesitated. Lisa had never mentioned it, but he knew it was her fervent hope that he would not follow in their father's path. He became aware that Pat McFee's offer to turn the dealer's chair over to him was meeting with something less than approval both at the stud table and surrounding games.

That decided Vance. "Thanks, Pat," he said. He walked to the vacated chair and slid into it.

"Cards, gentlemen," he said. "I'll bank the game for a while."

One of the players immediately got to his feet and shoved a few chips toward Vance. "I'm cashin' in," he said. "I don't like the smell of this place no longer."

Pat McFee stepped in and cashed the chips while Vance waited, the deck in his hand. The man who was quitting the game was Del Gilbert, one of the three ranchers Vance had tacitly accused of rustling Fitzroy calves in the past.

Del Gilbert turned to leave. "If you ride near my place tonight, Gilbert," Vance spoke, "better sing out and tell who you are. Bandy Plunkett's sleeping off a hangover there and he might be short on temper and quick on the trigger. The house was shot up last night. Bandy didn't like it. Didn't like it at all."

He added, "I didn't like it either."

Del Gilbert didn't answer. He pushed his way through the bystanders and left the Blue Star.

A man stepped up and took over the vacated chair. He was a stranger to Vance. "Do I buy chips?" he asked.

"Either way," Vance said. "Chips or cash. Blues

a dollar, reds four bits, whites two bits. Five-dollar limit on bets and raises."

The man bought thirty dollars worth of chips. He was a difficult person to classify. He wore a rather soiled white shirt with a snap-on black bow tie and a limp-brimmed range hat that shaded his eyes. His skin was weather-browned, and seemed to be a size or two too tight for the sharp, box-jawed structure of his face. He had a way of sitting with his narrow, high shoulders braced forward.

There was something vaguely familiar about him but Vance could not place the source in his mind. He definitely had the impression that here was a tough, keen-minded individual who could take care of himself.

The stranger, who said his name was Ed Walsh, shook hands all around, but did not mention where he came from, and it was not policy to ask. The other players at the table were cowhands who had come to town to watch the fun and were in no position, financially, to compete for stakes the size of those at other tables.

Vance also played carefully. The money he had flashed for Pop Rogers's benefit at the store had not been as ample as he had pretended. He was regretting now that he had failed to ride his lucky streak in San Antonio a trifle longer.

That luck now seemed to have deserted him. He lost two pots he believed he was certain to win. His stake was cut below twenty dollars. He backed into his shell, dropping out of hands early when his position was doubtful. Finally he caught aces, back-to-back, and made his opponents pay for their cards. He caught a third ace on the last card, with Ed Walsh backing two pairs.

That gave him chips with which to maneuver and bluff and feint. He began to forge steadily ahead. Two players decided they had enough, and cashed in, taking their losses. Two more men moved into the vacated seats. One was a big, loud-mouthed cattleman named Dolph Schneer who had been rolling it high at the dice table.

"Two hundred dollars in blues, Jardine," Schneer said as he sat down. He began scribbling an IOU on one of the slips of paper that he had brought with him.

"Cash only at this table," Vance said.

Schneer tossed the IOU toward him. "Let's have the chips," he said toughly. "I been waitin' fer a vacant seat at one of these poker tables fer an hour."

Vance ignored the paper. "Cash only," he repeated.

"Air you tryin' to say you don't think my IOU is worth what it says?" Schneer demanded.

"I wouldn't know," Vance said.

"So you wouldn't know? Let me tell you, Jardine, thet I had three hundred an' seventy-one head o' prime beef in the pool. Figger thet up at thirty-five dollars a head, then tell me my IOU ain't any good."

"It's good at other tables," Vance said patiently. "But not here. You know the rule at this table."

Schneer slapped a palm loudly on the table. "Did you hear that, boys?" he bawled, glaring around the room. "This here scum from the penitentiary don't think our money is any good."

Vance rose partly from his chair and swung a fist. Schneer went skidding back across the sawdust-covered floor, still seated in the chair. The chair capsized and Schneer skated beneath an adjoining poker table, upsetting another chair and a player. Both lay in a bug-like, leg-kicking tangle for a moment.

Schneer came to his knees. In his hand was a six-shooter. The man was drunk enough to have committed murder, and Vance was swung around, off-balance and in no position to draw his own weapon. He believed he was a dead man. Schneer could not miss at that close range.

Schneer did not fire. He let the pistol droop. He was staring, aghast, past Vance. Vance discovered that Ed Walsh, who had been sitting to his right, had a .45 leveled at Schneer. Walsh had appeared to be unarmed when he had sat into the poker game.

"Don't shoot!" Schneer gasped, suddenly sobered. "I was only foolin'."

Walsh did not answer. It occurred to Vance that he was debating whether to kill Schneer. There was in the man's long, bony face something utterly cold, utterly without pity. A lust was there—a lust to kill. Schneer must have seen that also.

Walsh's gun vanished as swiftly as it had appeared. "Get out!" he said. "You're delayin' this game."

Schneer scrambled to his feet. On his face, as he left the place hurriedly, was the awed expression of a man who felt that he had been looking down into his own grave, and had been spared.

Walsh turned to Vance. "Deal!" he said. There was no trace of emotion in his voice.

Vance flipped cards around the table. The other players dropped out on the first round, subdued by what they had witnessed. Vance's hole card was the ace of spades. His first up card was the eight in the same dark suit. Walsh had the eight of hearts showing.

Walsh bet a red chip. Vance called. It was a commonplace beginning of what was likely to be a small pot. Walsh caught the ace of diamonds on the second up card, Vance the eight of clubs, giving him a pair of eights showing. With the ace in the hole he had a big advantage, but he bet only two blues, baiting Walsh into revealing his own strength, or dropping out.

Walsh called the bet. That meant Walsh had a strong hole card also, or had hopes.

Vance had a curious premonition. He could almost have called beforehand the next cards they caught. Walsh's card was the ace of hearts, giving him a pair of aces, with an eight showing. Vance's card was also an ace. The ace of clubs. With the eight in the hole he now held aces and eights.

He met Walsh's eyes and saw a glint of cynical challenge in the man's stone cold gaze. He was certain now that Walsh's hole card was an eight. Walsh also held aces and eights. The red pairs.

Aces and eights. The dead man's hand. Legend had it that Wild Bill Hickok, the famous gunman, had held aces and eights when he had been murdered at a poker table in Deadwood. It was a superstition among poker players. Many men dropped out of a hand instantly on finding themselves with those cards.

Walsh, high on the table with his pair of aces, bet the limit, five blues. Vance called. He flipped the fifth card. He caught a king, Walsh a queen.

Walsh shrugged and shoved in his cards, conceding the pot. Vance had guessed correctly. Walsh had a red eight in the hole, but his fifth card, the queen, was beaten by Vance's king.

"I never saw two of 'em in the same deal before," Walsh said. "They tell me Hickok's aces and eights were black. Like yours, mister. Mine happened to be red."

Vance estimated the value of his pile of chips. "I'm cashing all of you in," he said, "and turning the deal back to Pat McFee."

After settling up with the players he was more than eighty dollars ahead. Pat McFee took over his chair, grinning and said, " 'Tis hoping you've left some of the luck, Vance me boy." He looked at the other players. "That was a horse on you boys, if you only knew it. Sure an' Vance was only playin' to win a birthday present for some of his small kinfolk so they wouldn't be afoot in the future on the way to school."

Ed Walsh arose, pushed his way through the bystanders and left the Blue Star without a word. "He is a hard man and a hard loser," Pat observed. "He is the kind that takes a thing like this as something to be remembered. He will not forget you, Vance."

"You know him?" Vance asked.

"I never laid eyes on him before tonight to my knowledge."

Vance drank a glass of beer at the bar, then moved to the street. The celebration was wilder than before. He lingered, watching, but never being a part of the merry-making. He felt that he never could become a part of it.

That again drove home the aching realization of what he had given up when he had taken the blame for Roy Carvell's misdeed. When the judge had sentenced him, he had also been sentenced to hover on the fringe of happiness, longing to grasp the reality of it, but always to be denied.

He knew the majority of these people, had grown up with many of them, danced with the young women at the range gatherings. Now, they avoided him, their eyes swinging quickly away when they identified him. Here and there among the older men he met open, ugly hostility. He realized that the story of his encounter with Dolph Schneer had gone around and how he had been backed by a gun-quick stranger.

Stacy Fitzroy was the life of the party, the queen of the ball. A waiting line of men was always on hand to take turns in dancing a few steps with her. She was vibrantly alive, flushed and deliriously happy.

Anger against them and their ostracism burned searingly again in Vance. He stayed on, stubborn and with a chip on his shoulder, daring them to knock it off. None did. At last he gave it up, his spirit burned out.

He returned to where he had left his horse and rode out of town, heading for his ranch. He had traveled some two miles when he sighted the glow of fire off to the south. The blaze seemed to be in the direction of Oak Hill, the Fitzroy ranch. He gigged his horse into a gallop, left the wagon trail and cut across country in that direction.

Reaching an elevation he could see the leap of the flames. Although the distance was still at least three miles it was apparent the main house was not involved. Some large out-building in the spread was burning.

He pushed his horse. Help would be needed, for a blaze of that size might spread to other structures. It was the stock shed, a long rambling structure that was used as a nursery for the strain of fine saddlehorses the major had developed, that was burning. The shed probably was not in use at this season, for Vance could see no evidence of any animals being involved as he emerged into close view of the ranch. Two smaller structures were also burning, a smokehouse and a grain crib.

The stock shed was a roaring pyre that had generated its own torrid whirlwind. There was little danger to the main house on its knoll a distance away, but the bunkhouse and other structures were likely to be involved. Three or four men were working frantically, dousing the bunkhouse and a wagonshed with water they were carrying in buckets from a windmill pond.

Vance spurred his horse in that direction, intending to join the bucket brigade. He yanked his horse back, for a wild figure, on foot, had appeared in its path. "Halt, or I'll shoot!" a man screeched.

Vance stared at the apparition. The figure in the torn, soot-stained nightshirt with a water-soaked towel wrapped around his head was the normally prim and lint-pick owner of Oak Hill—Major Webster Fitzroy.

Web Fitzroy had a cocked six-shooter in his hand and it was aimed at Vance's middle. Vance's first thought was that the fire had unbalanced the major's mind. His arms went rigidly into the air. For the second time within a few hours he expected to die.

"I saw the fire and was on my way to help!" he exclaimed. "Put down that gun! You know me. I'm—"

"I know you!" Web Fitzroy said hoarsely. "I know you only too well—you thief. You—you road agent. So you were in on it. I might have known."

"In on what?" Vance demanded.

"Where is it?" Web Fitzroy raged. "Where are the others? What have you done with it?"

"Done with what?" Vance demanded.

"The money!" Fitzroy almost screamed. "The beef money. More than one hundred thousand dollars."

Vance stared. "You don't mean—you *can't* mean it's gone?"

"You know it's gone! Stolen! And you know where it is!"

7

A woman, with a cloak over her nightdress, came hurrying. "Webster!" she cried. "Webster, darling! You shouldn't be here! You're hurt! What are you doing?"

Then she recognized Vance. She was Web Fitzroy's wife. Stacy's mother. Tall, distinguished in manner, she was from an aristocratic Southern family, and had been famed for her beauty when Web Fitzroy had wooed her and brought her to Del Rosa to preside over Oak Hill. She had lived in the shadow of her husband, carrying on the social duties at the ranch house.

Contrary to the attitudes of her husband and daughter, she had always shown Vance gentle courtesy whenever their paths had happened to cross on the trails or at range gatherings.

"I sighted the fire as I was heading from town to my place, ma'am," Vance explained. "I came to see if I could help. The major seems to think—"

"He was in on it, Amanda!" Web Fitzroy rasped. "He *must* have been. Why else would he have been skulking around here?"

Amanda Fitzroy tried to push down the gun her husband held. "You may be wrong, Webster," she said. "At least this is no time to shoot anyone."

Web Fitzroy kept the gun leveled. "We'll make

mighty certain whether I'm right or wrong!" he snapped. "Get off that horse, Jardine! Keep your hands up! Walk ahead of me—this way!"

"You're being hasty, darling," his wife protested.

Her husband ignored her. Vance slid from his horse and walked ahead of the ranch owner, his hands elevated. The stock shed collapsed with a great surge of flame that quickly subsided. The threat to the other structures was over.

The men who had been carrying water, halted, exhausted. They peered from smoke-reddened eyes and sooty faces. Vance saw that they were ranch hands.

"I caught this man skulking out in the brush," the major explained.

"Skulking aboard a horse that's been run hard for a couple of miles?" Vance jeered. "That, I'd like to see. Just how do you skulk with a horse that's blowing like a steam engine?"

He quit talking and stared at two men whose heads, like that of the major, were wrapped in water-soaked towels. One lay on a blanket and seemed dazed. The other was sitting up groggily. Vance knew them. The dazed man was Bob Archer who ran cattle east of Wolf Flat. The other, Jim O'Connor, owned a small spread in Little Round Valley.

"Would somebody please tell me what happened?" Vance asked.

Amanda Fitzroy seemed to be the only one composed enough to speak coherently. Her husband was stalking around, wringing his hands, shaking his fist at the stars, and uttering wild, unintelligible sounds.

"We woke up to find the shed burning," she said. "My husband and Mr. Archer and Mr. O'Connor were slugged by masked men as they rushed out of the house to fight the fire."

"Slugged?"

"With sandbags, evidently. I'm afraid poor Mr. Archer might be seriously injured. I've sent a rider to town to bring a doctor."

"What about the money? The beef money? The major said it was stolen?"

Web Fitzroy rushed at him, shaking a fist in his face. "You know that very well!" he shouted.

"Please, dear!" his wife pleaded. "You must be calm."

"Calm? Calm? When I've just been robbed of a hundred thousand dollars? When I've been made a fool of? When rascals try to burn down my beautiful, my lovely ranch house, and rob me of money that was in my trust? And you ask me to be calm!"

"I know, dear, how you feel. But you may be doing this young man an injustice. If he really had anything to do with what happened, it seems to me he would hardly have stayed around to be caught."

Web Fitzroy was in no mood to be reasoned with. He started to yell in fury, but his wife stiffened to her height and spoke sharply, "Simmer down, Webster! You're making a complete fool of yourself!"

Web Fitzroy seemed stunned. No person, not even his wife, was in the habit of offending his dignity in that manner.

She spoke to Vance. "The money has been stolen. The fire was set deliberately, no doubt. There were at least three men in on it. They were wearing black slickers and masks. They ran into the house after knocking my husband and the other two men unconscious. I came face-to-face with them as I rushed out of my bedroom. They pushed me back into the room. One said they would kill me if I made a sound. I heard them carry the boxes out. They went around the east corner of the house."

"Boxes?" Vance questioned.

"The money was in three Wells Fargo express boxes," she explained. "The kind used for carrying treasure."

"*Three* express boxes?"

"My husband had told me it was easier to handle, split up that way. A hundred thousand dollars in gold coin is very heavy."

"Did you recognize them? Could you identify them?"

"Don't answer that, Amanda!" her husband

roared. "He will find that out in court."

"I couldn't identify anyone," Amanda Fitzroy said. "I was the only person who even caught a glimpse of them, but they were too heavily masked. The men from the bunkhouse were busy fighting the fire and had no idea of what had happened until I came from the house. By that time I had heard horses leaving at a gallop. Many horses. It's my belief they had other men with them."

"Or maybe packhorses," Vance commented.

Web Fitzroy stared unbelievingly at his wife who had again defied his order not to talk. "I don't understand you, Amanda!" he thundered.

Riders came pouring into the ranch yard. The blaze had been sighted from town. Wagons and buggies joined the incoming stream. Two doctors arrived and took charge of the major and the other two men. Their injuries, apparently, were not too serious.

"How come there were only these three men in the house?" Vance asked Amanda Fitzroy.

The major was still keeping a gun in his hand, and watching grimly, but his wife seemed to feel she could talk freely to Vance.

"Originally there were six men, including my husband, who guarded the money all the way from Platte City," she said. "They came by train as far as San Antonio. That took nearly a week, because they had to change trains several times, and there were long waits now and then. They hired a stagecoach at San Antonio to bring them the rest of the way home. They reached the ranch late the night before last. They stayed there rather than go on into town after midnight. My husband sent word the next morning to Mayor Jim Thomas."

"You say there had been *six* men?"

"My husband decided there was no longer any need for so many to guard the boxes here at Oak Hill, and let three of the ranchers return to their homes yesterday. After all, they hadn't seen their families for months. Only Mr. Archer and Mr. O'Connor stayed to help my husband keep watch."

"That was yesterday. Why did they stay at the ranch? Why didn't they take the money on into town?"

"Jim Thomas rode out to Oak Hill to ask my husband to delay the arrival in town until a proper welcome and celebration could be arranged. That, unfortunately, seemed to have given the thieves time to plan the robbery."

"Who were the three who went home?"

"John Clay, Frank Smith and Case Quinn," she said slowly. She added, "I know what you're thinking. But they are solid, honest ranchers. My husband picked them as guards of the money because he was sure he could depend on them. He feels that none of them had anything to do with the robbery."

Neither spoke for a time. Amanda Fitzroy waited. It struck Vance that she seemed to be expecting something of him. Advice, perhaps. Or at least a clear mind, something the major was obviously in no condition to furnish.

"It took more than six men to handle a drive of three thousand head on a long haul like that," he said.

"Yes. There were eight others. They are coming home, saddleback, bringing the chuckwagon and such of the saddle strings as weren't sold at Platte City. My husband said they probably would not pull in for two or three weeks."

Vance became aware of a change in the situation in the ranch yard. At first the arrivals had been too appalled to do more than stand speechless and despairing when they learned their good fortune had vanished.

Anger was now rising. They began shouting their disbelief. They surrounded the major, snarling and yelling, accusing him of careless cowardice. Their mood swung from ugly to vicious.

A new arrival on horseback, spurred through the group. It was Stacy Fitzroy on a winded mount. She swung down. "What's this?" she demanded.

Her arrival silenced the threats while Amanda Fitzroy explained the situation. Stacy turned and stared scornfully at the bystanders.

"You've got some explainin' to do, major," someone in the crowd yelled out. "You've

102

always been Billy-Big around here. Now, you've lost the money that was comin' to us. What air you goin' to do about it?"

Others joined in the demand. Web Fitzroy tried to speak, but could not make himself heard. Sheriff Bill Summers arrived and listened to the charges and countercharges. He glared at Web Fitzroy. "How about it, Fitzroy?" he demanded. "I want to talk to you alone. Meanwhile, a lot of you boys git ready to ride posse."

Stacy Fitzroy placed herself in the sheriff's path. "To you, Bill Summers," she said, "my father's name is *Major* Fitzroy. Keep that in mind in addressing him."

Bill Summers wilted a trifle. "Yes'm," he said meekly.

But Web Fitzroy, in his bandage and bedraggled nightshirt, was not the picture of the dignity he had always presented in the past. He was haggard, bewildered, confused by the yapping chorus of ranchers who had been acclaiming him only a few hours earlier.

Vance located his horse and mounted. He looked back as he rode away. Amanda Fitzroy and Stacy were at the major's side. Web Fitzroy's plight reminded him of a drawing some bar room artist had painted of a blizzard-bound, old, buffalo bull, surrounded by wolves that were closing in for the kill.

Daybreak was still hours away when he

unsaddled at his ranch. Bandy awakened when he entered the house, and listened as Vance told him what had happened.

Bandy punctuated the recital with groans and gasps of incredulity. "There's sure goin' to be ol' Satan to pay, an' he'll want it spiked on a hot pitchfork," he predicted. "More'n a hundred thousand simoleons. In gold! Halfway to Mexico by this time, most likely. Web Fitzroy would have been better off if he'd cashed in with a busted skull."

"It can't be as bad as that."

"You've heard of what goeth before a fall, haven't you? Pride. Well, Web Fitzroy's had his fall. It ain't the first one, but this time it'll likely be fatal. If you ask me, it's only justice that the conceit be taken out of him."

"They can't blame it all on him," Vance said.

"They kin an' will. He's snooted his neighbors all his life, tried to make 'em believe the sun rose an' set at Oak Hill fer the 'special benefit o' the Fitzroys. Now, it's their turn. I give him credit fer ramroddin' the drive an' fer ketchin' the beef market at a high price, but they'll forgit that now, an' try to pick his bones."

"I feel sorry for him," Vance admitted.

"You ought to be the last to say that, seein' as how he'd tried to grind you Jardines under his heel all these years."

Vance shrugged. "All he ever got was a

blistered heel. We don't grind easy. At that, I never figured out why he had it in for us."

"I just told you. Pride. Sometimes that's another name for envy. Jealousy."

"Envy? Jealousy? The major? What are you talking about?"

"Your paw was everything the major wanted to be, but wasn't. He never forgave him fer that."

"Now you must be loco to say a thing like that," Vance said.

"Who was it that went away to war as a private in the ranks, an' come back a cavalry captain with a lot of battle stripes an' a decoration for gallantry that was pinned on him by none other than General Robert E. Lee in person? Not the major. The major went to war a major, havin' enough political power to git the title. He come back a major. The nearest he ever got to a cannonball was when he was seein' 'em turned out in the iron foundries at Birmingham, Alabama. That was where he spent the war. He was a supply officer."

Bandy added, before Vance could speak, "No, I ain't sayin' the major lacked sand. He was more valuable to the Cause where they sent him, for he's got a talent for figures an' production—like the way he handled the beef drive. An' it wasn't your fault your paw come home from the war the same day the major was bein' welcomed back at a big hurrah the politicians had fixed up."

105

"It just couldn't have happened that way," Vance groaned.

"But it did. I was there. I came home with your paw. There was to have been a parade, an' speeches. The shindig had just started when Silkhat Jack Jardine an' me rode into town. He wasn't wearin' a silk hat that day. That came later. We'd traveled all the way from Tennessee, where we'd been mustered out, an' we was sort of ragged, an' hadn't put on any fat at all. There was the major sittin' on the speakers' stand, along with the big-wigs, him in his fancy, tailored major's uniform, with a sash an' a sword he'd never been called on to draw. An' there was Captain Jack Jardine in patched, washed-out Confederate gray, who didn't know what all the cheerin' was about. The cheerin' was for him. Everybody forgot all about the major. It was your paw's return they celebrated."

"Is that why the major had it in for my father?"

"There was other reasons. Yore paw was the best pistol shot, the best rifle shot in the Del Rosa. The major was next best. Yore paw was a natural born gambler. A chance-taker. The major never did a thing in his life without circlin' around it, studyin' it from every side beforehand. He *wanted* to be a gambler, but it jest wasn't in his nature. He was afeared of only one thing."

"What was that?"

"Afeared he'd make a mistake that would

106

make people laugh at him. He likely could stand torture without turnin' a hair, but to be made to look foolish, like the day they forgot about him an' whooped it up for yore father, was somethin' he never could forgit, nor forgive. Now, a bunch o' thieves has made a fool of him ag'in—at least in his own eyes. To add to it, the son of Captain Jack Jardine turns out to be a hero too, even though he was sent to prison. It's like history repeatin' itself. An' yore maw did mortal hurt to the major before you was born because she didn't take his conceit seriously, an' run away to elope with a gambler. She was the purtiest girl in these parts, an', as such, the major considered that she should have married him."

"But the major has a fine wife," Vance said.

"Nobody, least of all me, has ever said different. Amanda Fitzroy is the salt o' the earth. An' as purty as was yore mother, which is sayin' *somethin'*. It took the major quite some time to find one that good-lookin' so he could fetch her home as his wife an' parade her so as to try an' make folks believe he'd got the best o' Jack Jardine after all. If Amanda Fitzroy made a mistake in marryin' Web Fitzroy, she never gave any sign of it. She's the kind that will stand by a bargain to the finish. She's a real lady—the sort that don't wear their breedin' like a banner.

"Stacy looks a lot like her mother but it's her father who taught her to believe she's better'n everyone else. He's raised her to be high-nosed like himself. Now, I reckon, she'll have to eat humble pie along with him."

"That will be something neither of us will ever see," Vance said. "The major might have been thrown from his high horse, but his daughter never will be."

"Stacy's got spunk, that's fer sure. I recollect that you used to pester the life out o' her when you was school kids."

"I can't say she got the worst of it," Vance said. "She could throw rocks like a sharpshooter. I've got a few scars on my skull to prove it."

"She had plenty of cause to have it in for you," Bandy said. "I wonder why she used to ride by here, now an' then, while you were away."

"Stacy Fitzroy used to come by here? What for?"

"Maybe she just wanted somebody to talk to. Talk is one of my strong points when I'm of a mind."

"You do have a tendency for it," Vance said.

"The major's kept her away from the common herd so much of her life, maybe she just wanted to try to get back into it now an' then. She asked me once in a while what I'd heard about you. Maybe she only wanted to make sure you were still penned up. On the other hand she mentioned once that she didn't believe you had ever held up any stagecoach at all, an' that you must have—"

Bandy broke off. A rider was approaching. A small, frightened voice called, "Uncle Vance! Uncle Vance! Are you there?"

Vance rushed out. Little Chad Carvell was astride a big saddle, with his bare feet thrust through the stirrup leathers. He wore breeches with his nightshirt stuffed in. The horse had been hard-ridden.

Vance lifted the boy from the saddle. "What's wrong?"

Chad started to speak, looked at Bandy and thought better of it. He was fighting back tears. Bandy understood and backed out of hearing.

"It's Dad, Uncle Vance," Chad choked. "I want you to come. He's hurt."

"Hurt? How?"

"I don't know. I just don't know. Please get your horse and go back with me. Mother needs help."

"Your mother's with him? Is she all right?"

"Yes. She told me to stay in bed and go to sleep. But I didn't. I know she needs help. I think we're in terrible trouble, Uncle Vance."

"Why didn't you ride for a doctor?"

Chad could no longer fight back the sobbing. He didn't answer that. Vance had a sudden freezing hunch he knew the reason.

He called to Bandy, "Catch me up my horse. I've got to ride over to Lisa's. Somebody's been taken sick."

Bandy asked no questions. While he was roping and rigging the horse, Vance ran to the house and reached for his holstered gun which hung on the wall. He paused. On second thought, he let the weapon remain there. He returned to the yard unarmed.

He swung Chad back on his horse and started to mount. Bandy caught his arm. "One time was enough, boy," Bandy murmured. "Roy Carvell was bad medicine to you once before."

Vance sighed and mounted. "So long," he said. He spoke to Chad. "Hang on, old-timer, we're going to split the wind."

They headed across range in the starlight. Daybreak was still an hour or more away. "What happened?" Vance asked the boy.

Chad had steadied. "All I know is I woke up a long time after I'd gone to sleep an' heard riders arrivin' at the barn. I fell asleep again, for I thought it was Dad an' some of the boys. I woke up again. There was some cussin' at the barn. Then a shot was fired. I jumped out o' bed in time to see two men in slickers ridin' away into the brush."

"Your mother?"

"She screamed when she heard the shot an' ran out. I followed her, but she told me to go back to bed. I didn't. I hid alongside the barn. Mom found Dad in there in the dark. He was hurt, for he was groanin'. She wanted to take him to the house, but he told her to hide him out somewhere. She said she'd send me to fetch a doctor, but he didn't want that either. His horse was standin' near, still saddled, so I rode to git you."

"How about Fern?"

"She slept through it all," Chad said. He added, "After all, she's only a little girl."

Vance asked no more questions. Daylight was on the horizon when he eased the pace and approached the shabby ranch at Whisky Ford. The house was dark and silent, but he was sure he had seen a glimmer of light in the barn at first sight from a distance. It, too, was dark and silent now, a black shape brooding in the shadow of dawn.

Vance rode to its open wagon gate. "Lisa?" he called guardedly. "It's Vance. Are you in there?"

"Vance!" Lisa came out of the blackness of the interior. She looked at Chad on the tired horse and began to sob. "Oh, Chad! I told you not to—"

"Is Roy in there?" Vance asked. "Chad said he was hurt."

"Go home, brother," Lisa said huskily. "Chad should never have brought you here. He didn't understand. Go home! Please!"

Roy Carvell's voice, weak and pain-ridden, came out of the darkness. "I've got a bullet in me, Vance. You got to help me. Lisa faints every time she sees a little blood."

Vance dismounted and started to enter the barn. His sister threw her arms around him, holding him back. "No!" she said imploringly. "I won't let you. I know what you did before. I wouldn't let myself admit it for a long time. I won't let you get mixed up in anything like that again."

"I'm goin' to die if somebody don't help me," Roy Carvell moaned. "I'm bleedin' to death, Vance."

"I'll be all right, Lisa," Vance said. "I can't ride away and let you alone with this. You know that."

He drew free of her arms and moved into the darkness. Fumbling for his matches, he struck a light. Roy Carvell was lying on a blanket. An oil lamp stood on the floor nearby. Its chimney was still warm when Vance touched it. He relighted the lamp and replaced the chimney.

Roy was ashen. His shirt had been cut from him. A stained bandage was wrapped around his chest.

Lisa and Chad had followed Vance. He spoke to Chad. "Better go to the house and keep Fern from being scared in case she wakes up, old-timer. I'll call you if we need help."

Chad reluctantly obeyed. Vance looked at Lisa. "How bad? How deep?"

"I don't know," she said shakily. "The bullet is still in Roy. I could feel it on his side, toward the back."

Vance opened the bandage which had been torn from a sheet. He held the lamp close, peering. At his request, Lisa brought water and more cloths. He washed away the blood.

Roy watched with frightened eyes. He had been drinking, but his plight had sobered his mind. "I ain't goin' to die, am I?" he croaked.

"No such luck," Vance said.

"My God, Vance, ain't you got any pity? Promise me one thing. If I die, I want you to see to it that Len Kelso an' his pardner hang for it, the dirty, double-crossin' rats."

Vance said, "Shut up! You're only making this thing bleed better. Lisa, fetch Roy's razor. And anything else that might help in digging out a bullet. It's stuck just under his hide along a rib. Fetch a needle and thread. Linen thread, if you have it."

Lisa hurried to the house to obey. "It'll hurt!" Roy almost sobbed. "It'll hurt terrible, won't it?"

"You won't enjoy it," Vance said.

"I can't stand pain. Find some whisky. Put me under. My jug's empty."

"You're bleeding mainly alcohol already."

"You're a hard man, Vance. All I ask is that you see to it that Len Kelso an' his pal pay for it, if'n I die. It was that devil Len brought along that shot me."

"You'll live to take care of your own snakes," Vance said. "Quit blubbering."

113

Lisa returned with implements. Vance swabbed away the blood and used the razor. Roy uttered a howl. Vance jammed a knee on him and held him down while he used needle and thread, closing the incision.

He finally moved back. Roy lay moaning. Lisa leaned faintly against the wall of a stall, fighting off nausea.

"You can bandage him up again," Vance said.

He picked up a bullet from the floor and tossed it on Roy's chest. "Here's a souvenir. You were lucky, that time. That slug must have been slowed down by a button or something. It glanced along a rib. All you really got is a gouge. You'll be in shape in a few days to get into more trouble, I'm afraid."

He waited until Lisa had completed the bandage. "You better go to see how Chad and Fern are getting along," he said.

She understood that he wanted to talk to her husband alone. She came close to him and whispered tensely, "He's done something wrong again, of course. I don't want to know what it is, but I do want you to leave. You must not get involved again, brother."

Vance kissed her. "Go to the house, dear."

She reluctantly complied. He snuffed the lamp. "We can talk in the dark," he said to Roy. "You fool! Don't you know you could get twenty years for what you did tonight. Maybe life. You and your pals held up Oak Hill ranch and tried to burn it down in the bargain. In addition to that you slugged three men."

"I was drunk," Roy moaned. "They badgered me into it."

"The same way Len Kelso badgered you into sticking up that stage a couple years ago, and left you to hang and rattle. Who was in this with you and Len?"

"I don't know."

"What do you mean, you don't know?"

"He said his name was Sam Jones. I never laid eyes on him 'til we met here at the barn early tonight an' headed fer Oak Hill. He didn't do much talkin'. Len had pestered me into it the other afternoon. Said it'd be a cinch an' we'd git rich. I know now it was this Sam Jones who'd figgered out the whole scheme. He seemed to be a stranger around here, for he didn't know anything about the country. Len took care of that part of it, but it was Sam Jones that gave all the orders."

"What did this Sam Jones look like?"

"I didn't git too much of a peek at him. It was dark, an' he kept his hat pulled low. We all put on slickers an' masks when we got near Oak Hill."

"Where would they be heading?"

"Mexico, most likely," Roy said. "That was where we was all supposed to go."

"Just the three of you were in on this?"

"That's right."

"How many pack horses?"

"Three. One for each box. Sam Jones said we'd need that many so as to travel fast. Len furnished the pack animals. Sam Jones was right. Them boxes was mighty heavy. I never figured on money weighin' that much."

"Three riders and three pack animals would make a trail a blind man could follow to this ranch," Vance snapped.

"We figgered that out beforehand. I cut west. Len an' Sam Jones headed north. We all come into the San'tone stage trail at different points before midnight, follered it in this direction. There are two night stage runs that pass along that road after midnight, one eastbound, the other west. There ain't a trailer in the Del Rosa, not even Juan Sonora, who'd be able to puzzle out any tracks after two six-horse teams had chopped up the dust."

"And you all met here?"

"Yeah. That was when I made my mistake," Roy said. "I busted open them Fargo boxes before I was supposed to. Sam Jones an' Len had gone out to scout around. I couldn't wait. I pried off the hasps of the boxes. So Sam Jones shot me."

"They took the money with them when they pulled out, of course?" Vance said.

Roy uttered a cackle of mirthless laughter. "What money?"

"The money in the Fargo boxes," Vance snapped. "What else? A hundred thousand dollars, give or take."

Roy again laughed with bitter irony. "Just a leetle, old hundred thousand, huh? Damn all their smart, schemin' souls!"

"Get some iron in your backbone, for once, Roy," Vance said. "If you help recover that money, you'd likely get off easy. People in the Del Rosa would forgive a lot if they had their hands on that beef money."

"That'd be real kind of 'em," Roy snarled. " 'Specially of the major. The crook!"

"Quit stalling. The sooner we get on the trail of those two the better chance we've got of getting those Fargo boxes back. You must have some idea of where they intended to head. Mexico, I suppose?"

"If it's only the Fargo boxes you want," Roy spat, "you needn't do any ridin'. They're here."

Vance stared. "Are you saying the money's still here? In this barn?"

"The three boxes are," Roy sneered. "An' every bit of what was in 'em."

"What are you trying to say? Talk, man! Talk fast! I'm not as sure as you that somebody won't pick up your trail and show up here any minute."

A man spoke in the shadows back of them.

"We have already arrived, *señors*. Raise your arms, *Señor* Jardine. If you try to move we will be forced to shoot you."

The voice was that of the Yaqui, Juan Sonora. Vance stood empty of all emotion, except that of bitter protest. For the second time he was involved in a crime his brother-in-law had committed.

Daybreak had strengthened enough so that he knew he would be an easy target. "All right," he said, and lifted his hands. "I'm not armed."

"Search him to make sure, Juan," the thin, quivering voice of a girl spoke. "And Carvell too. I'll keep them covered."

It was Stacy Fitzroy!

8

Vance turned, astounded. "You stand still!" Stacy Fitzroy warned shrilly. She was grasping a cocked six-shooter with both hands.

Vance tried to bluff it out. "Put that thing down before you shoot yourself by accident, like Roy did."

Juan Sonora chuckled ironically as he made sure neither Vance nor Roy Carvell had weapons. Evidently Lisa had taken Roy's pistol away.

"An accident was it?" Stacy Fitzroy said jeeringly. "You surely aren't soft-headed enough to try to protect your brother-in-law a second time, Vance Jardine? We've been out there for some time, listening."

"You seem to have a talent for snooping around and horning in on private conversations," Vance said.

"And lucky for you, my friend. I saw Len Kelso sneaking away from this barn the other afternoon. You saw him too, I imagine. The minute I learned how the money had been stolen, I felt sure he and your brother-in-law were in on it. I talked Juan into coming here with me, just on the hunch we might have a better chance of learning something, rather than having that big-mouthed sheriff come roaring here with a posse and stampeding the robbers out of the country."

Daylight was seeping into the barn. Lisa appeared in the wide doorway and stood peering, white-faced.

Stacy sighed. "See what you've done?" she said to Roy Carvell. "Hasn't she had it tough enough, without you adding this to her troubles?"

She met Lisa. There were tears and sobbing, but she prevailed on Lisa to return to the house.

"Now!" she said to Carvell when she returned. "Exactly where is the money?"

Roy answered that with another of his bitter cackles of laughter. "What money?" he asked.

Stacy stamped a foot. "The express boxes you men took from Oak Hill. I heard you say they were still here in this barn."

A sly, triumphant note entered Roy Carvell's voice. "Let's go over this, dearie," he snickered. "Your father says there was a hundred thousand dollars in them boxes, didn't he? Right?" Vance decided that a new thought had entered Roy's mind which he believed gave him an advantage.

Juan Sonora nudged Roy with the muzzle of a pistol. "Do what the *señorita* asks," he warned. "Tell her where is the *dinero*! And speak with respect."

"Just what would happen if your paw didn't get back that beef money?" Roy asked Stacy. "He was responsible for it, wasn't he? Them other boys will sort of insist that he make good, won't they?"

"What are you driving at?" she said angrily.

"Talk sense, Roy!" Vance snapped. "Quit stalling! We all heard you say the money was here."

Roy continued to address Stacy Fitzroy. "I was always sure there was a thief back o' that stuffed shirt Web Fitzroy put on every mornin' to fool people."

"Thief?" she exclaimed indignantly. "What are you up to? What do you mean?"

"I'll show you what I mean," Roy sneered. "Give me a hand, Vance. Help me on my feet." More than ever he seemed to feel that he was in command of the situation.

Vance eyed him with contempt. "Get on your feet yourself," he said. "You don't need help. And make it mighty fast. I'm losing my patience."

Vance prodded him with the toe of his boot, and Roy arose quickly to his feet.

Roy moved across the barn. Vance lighted the lamp. Roy led the way to a cluttered corner and threw back the cover on a big, dusty sheetiron box where grain for feed had once been stored. The box had not been used in years, evidently.

Three ironbound, wooden chests of the familiar type used for treasure shipments lay there. They bore the scarred, painted name of Wells Fargo. Their locks had been pried off, the lead seals broken.

"Here's your danged beef money," Roy said, and threw back the lids.

Vance peered down at the contents of the treasure boxes. He turned and gazed, unbelievingly at his companions. What they were looking at were rusty iron horseshoes, old wagon bolts, common riverbed stones and other worthless items.

Stacy Fitzroy pressed close to him as she peered. Juan Sonora covered his mouth with his hand to hide an impolite gasp of amazement.

There was no sound for moments. Vance finally turned to his brother-in-law. Roy Carvell was grinning with malicious triumph.

"What is this?" Vance asked.

"You can see it," Roy said. "You're not blind, are you?"

"Where's the money?"

Roy addressed Stacy Fitzroy. "Maybe you better ask that question of your father."

Again the silence. Finally she spoke slowly. "Are you insinuating that my father removed the money from these chests for his own profit and replaced it with this stuff?"

"I ain't implyin' it," Roy spat. "I'm sayin' it right out an' out. Web Fitzroy is a slick thief."

Stacy Fitzroy was too confused to speak for a space. She finally said hollowly, "You're lying.

You and your pals took the money and filled the boxes with this junk."

She added, "I see it now. Your purpose is to try to divert guilt from yourself and throw suspicion on my father."

Juan Sonora jammed the muzzle of his gun into Roy's teeth, bringing a trickle of blood from a split lip. "Tell us the truth!" Juan Sonora said. "Or I weel knock out all thees teeth, one by one."

Roy's arrogance vanished. He recoiled from the Yaqui in terror. "That's what we found in the boxes," he gurgled. "I swear it."

Stacy Fitzroy intervened, pushing the Yaqui back. "No, Juan!" she said. "Let him talk." She glared at Roy. "Are you telling the truth?"

"So God help me!" Roy mumbled.

Vance suddenly felt sure his brother-in-law, for once, was not lying. Stacy Fitzroy evidently was convinced also. Then the Fitzroy pride and self-assurance returned. "Your two pals took the gold and filled the boxes with this trash," she said.

"Impossible," Roy said. "For one thing, I had one of the boxes with me from the minute we carried them out of Oak Hill. Len an' Sam Jones had the other two, but they just couldn't have changed the contents. It'd have been impossible. That gold was taken out of them Fargo boxes while they was layin' in a room at Oak Hill, if you ask me."

She spoke to Juan Sonora. "We'll find the sheriff and turn him over. He's lying, of course."

"How about thees one?" Juan Sonora asked, indicating Vance.

She shrugged. "It'd only be a waste of time. In addition to having an alibi, having been in town miles away when all this started, he's got you and me as witnesses that he came here tonight only because his sister needed help."

"You sort of change with every turn of the wheel," Vance commented. "Seems to me not long ago you just couldn't remember having seen me in town."

"My memory might fail me again," she said. "In court, perhaps, if need be."

"You ain't turnin' me over to no sheriff," Roy spoke.

"Why not?" she asked.

"How's it goin' to set with all them ranchers in the beef pool when they find out what was really in them treasure boxes?"

"They wouldn't dare suspect my father!" she said grimly.

Roy laughed knowingly. "Now, wouldn't they? You Fitzroys ain't been exactly the best-liked folks in these parts. A hundred thousand dollars is enough to tempt any man. It's a lot more'n Oak Hill is worth the way things are."

"Ridiculous!" Stacy lashed back.

"Is it now? Maybe people will figure the major

knew more about the holdup than he told. Fact is, I'm beginnin' to wonder myself if it wasn't a put-up job between him an' this mysterious Sam Jones, an' that I was played for a sucker."

There was a long silence. Stacy Fitzroy stood silent, her lower lip held in her teeth, thinking. Vance understood that she was caught in a very awkward situation.

"You slimy worm," she said to Roy. "You—you—!" She couldn't find the words to express her contempt. Roy began breathing freely again. His sly grin returned. He knew he had made his point. He held the whiphand.

"Take that gun out of my backbone," he said to Juan Sonora. "I ain't goin' nowhere I don't want to go."

"Do you really think you can get off that easy?" Stacy demanded.

Roy spread his hands in a mocking gesture. "I've got nothin' personal ag'in the major. I'd be the last person in the world to mention that he might have cached that money somewhere, then framed up a fake robbery."

Defeat was bitter for Stacy Fitzroy. She stood there for a time trying to plan something that would wipe away Roy's twisted smile. She seemed defeated. Then her expression changed. She turned and pinned Vance with her eyes. "I want to talk to you," she said.

Vance backed away from her. "It takes two to

hold a talk," he said. "I've got nothing to say to you."

"But I'm sure you have," she said sweetly. "Or would you prefer about ten more years in Huntsville? It would go hard for a man to come up a second time on a holdup charge, even though he had been pardoned on the first conviction. Ten years would be about the least you'd get, I imagine."

Vance glared at her. "What sort of a person are you? Do you know the penalty for perjury?"

"Hu—ump!" she grunted. "Come to think of it, I wonder if you didn't actually have a hand in this thing. I believe I heard it mentioned in town last night that you refused to accept IOUs from ranchers who had money in the beef pool. Maybe you had reason to know those IOUs would be worthless. In other words, a jury might be convinced, even without any testimony from me, that you had previous knowledge there would be a holdup at Oak Hill. Did you?"

"Of course not! You know as well as I do that—"

"I believe it would be well if we discussed this further—just the two of us. Follow me."

Vance followed her out of earshot of Carvell and Juan Sonora. "I've got a feeling," he said, "that I'm being blackmailed."

"That," she said lightly, "is perhaps the correct, ugly term for it."

"Just what do you want?"

"I? See here, Mister Vance Jardine, are you suggesting that you may try to force me into some kind of a deal with you?"

"*Me?* Force *you* into a deal?"

"Exactly. Are you trying to intimidate me so as to prevent me from exposing your brother-in-law, and to keep me quiet about any part you may have played in this robbery on the threat that you might bring false charges against my father that might injure his reputation?"

Vance drew a long, helpless breath. "Say that again," he said. "Slower and clearer."

"You heard me," she said. "You seem to be trying to force me to keep silent as the price of your own silence."

Vance removed his hat and bowed elaborately. "I got to give you credit, Anastasia," he said. "You ought to go in for trading horses. You're wasting your time trying to blackmail a patch-saddle rancher like me with hardly a cent to his name."

"I don't know what you are trying to say," she replied.

"The deal you're trying to bulldoze me into is that if you scratch my back, I'll scratch yours," Vance said.

"A vulgar way of putting it," she said.

"What do you want of me?"

"Why, nothing at all," she replied. She added,

as though it was an afterthought, "Of course we will keep all the details of this little matter between the four of us. I can speak for Juan. I trust you will see to it that your brother-in-law keeps his lying mouth closed."

"I'm sure he'd be the last one to want to talk about it," Vance said. "So that's the deal you're putting over? Do we shake on it?"

She smiled icily. "That won't be necessary. And no back-scratching either."

"What about the sheriff?" Vance asked. "He might come nosing around here. Will you keep him off Roy?"

"Of course not," she said. "That's his problem." She seemed suddenly exhausted. She had turned the tables on Roy and Vance, forced them to accept her terms. Now the Fitzroy pride was no longer sufficient to conceal the fact that she was not as sure of herself as she pretended. She was shaking.

She indicated the express boxes. "What will you do with them? They must be hidden. And in a better place."

"I'll see to it," Vance said. "You are a wicked person."

"Indeed I am," she said. "And there'll be no end to my wickedness when it comes to protecting my father. I happen to love him very much. He had nothing to do with this. He believed the money was in those express boxes.

I'm sure of that. I know him too well to believe anything else."

Vance remained silent. She took that as cynical disagreement. "He has promised to make restitution to the others," she said. "He will keep his word. It would mean selling the ranch. He would lose everything."

Vance still said nothing. He could have pointed out that if her father had substituted the contents of the treasure box he was still one hundred thousand dollars ahead, a sum worth far more than Oak Hill under the circumstances and sufficient to stake a new life somewhere else.

Her mind seemed to sense the run of his thoughts. "I tell you he's innocent!" she exclaimed. She added, "I want to see you again."

"About what?"

"I'm not sure," she said. "But you don't imagine that you and I are through with all this, do you?"

"I was certainly hoping so."

"Well, we're not."

"I was afraid there'd be a string on the deal you made."

"I'll come over to your ranch tonight, if possible, for a longer talk. If not tonight, then the next night I can make it. I want to go over this again with my father. Maybe I can have some idea as to what really happened."

"I can't say I'm interested," Vance said.

"You've got to be," she said grimly. "I might need help, and I've a belief you're the one who can furnish it."

"More blackmail?"

"Let's just call it more back-scratching," she said. "Wait for me at your place, each night."

Juan Sonora had brought up their horses. She and the Yaqui mounted and rode away into the brush along the stream, heading in the direction of Oak Hill.

Vance found a pick and shovel in the barn. Working fast, he dug a hole in a box stall, deep enough to hold the express boxes. He carried the heavy boxes into the stall, covered them with earth which he tamped and tramped. He spread old straw and residue over the spot and turned Roy's horse into the stall, forking in more straw, and filled the feed rack with hay.

He rubbed the horse down to hide any evidence it had been ridden during the night. Roy watched the operation. "What if'n they come nosin' around here?" Roy groaned. "That box stall might be the first place they'd think about."

"And maybe the last," Vance said. "It isn't every day I have to hide a collection of scrap iron in a hurry. I can't take a chance on being caught in daylight lugging this stuff out into the brush. Someone might show up any minute."

"How about me? Where'll I hide?"

"Nowhere. You stay right here at your place, as

usual. Wear your shirt. Put on a brush jacket if anybody shows up. Can you use that left arm at all?"

"Some. But it hurts like hell."

"Let it hurt. Pretend you're all right. Nobody has any reason to suspect you, but they'll begin to wonder if you or anybody else turns up missing. If Len Kelso is really heading for Mexico, you better pray he makes it. If he's caught, he'll talk, and you'll be in the soup. Exactly why did his partner shoot you?"

"He got mad because I busted the boxes open. He said not to waste time openin' them 'til later. He got a lot madder when he saw that we'd gone to all that trouble just to carry off a lot of scrap iron. I busted open the boxes while him an' Len had gone out to scout around."

Lisa returned and had been listening to all this. She now knew everything. Vance put an arm around her. "Send the kids off to school today, as usual," he said. "Tell Chad not to say a word about last night, not even to Fern. Do you think he'll heed?"

She nodded, dry-eyed. "He'll do anything if I tell him you asked it. He likes you. He takes after you."

The sun was coming up. Vance mounted. "I'll try to keep out of the way of any possemen," he said. "They might want to know why I'm heading home at sunup."

He made the ride back to his place on Rock Creek without encountering any manhunters. Bandy was awake and took care of the horse. Bandy asked no questions. He slapped slabs of bacon into the skillet, added slices of potatoes and two eggs, and warmed biscuits.

Vance cleaned his plate and drank black coffee. "I'm going to turn in for a few hours," he said casually. "I'd appreciate it if you'd let me know in case someone comes poking around."

He grinned tiredly at Bandy and added, "Nope, I didn't shoot anybody or rob any ranches. But I did bump into as slick a horse trader as I've ever tried to buck, and I've got the hunch I'm going to get the worst of it before long."

He headed for a bunk in the adjoining room. "By the way, if this horse trader happens to show up, wake me up. But I don't believe there's much chance she'll pull in until after nightfall at least, if at all."

"She?" Bandy barked, his brows arching.

But Vance was heading for the bunk and fell asleep without explaining.

9

Bandy awakened him at noon. "We got visitors!" Bandy announced. "The shurrif, an' a lot of gents with guns stickin' out like the quills on a porcupine." He added, "There's not a female in the lot."

Vance pulled on his boots, dashed water on his face at the wash bench, used the towel Bandy handed him. They walked out to meet more than half a dozen riders who came up on dusty horses and dismounted in the ranch yard without awaiting the customary invitation to alight.

Bill Summers was saddle-galled and sour-minded. Vance had the impression the sheriff was close to total confusion. The officer was confronted with the biggest responsibility of his career and evidently found himself beyond his depth.

George Klink and Dolph Schneer were among the possemen. Schneer had a swollen jaw as a memento of his collision with Vance's fist recently. George Klink had never forgotten that Vance had named him as a brand blotter. Both men were savagely anxious to pay off their grudges.

"What can I do for you men?" Vance asked.

The sheriff brushed past him and stalked into

the house, followed by Klink and Schneer. They began ransacking the place, dragging blankets and sheets off the bunks, snatching garments from the hangers. They overturned chairs, and yanked out drawers, spilling the contents on the floor.

"All right!" Bill Summers finally snarled. "If he was in on it, he's been smart enough to have hid any evidence."

They turned to stalk out. What they had really come for was to water and feed their horses at the creek and the haystack Bandy had harvested from the meadows of wild hay along the stream. They had given in to the temptation to commit vandalism.

"Hold it!" Vance said.

They found themselves looking into the bore of the .45 that had been hanging in a holster on the wall.

They halted, sucking in startled sighs. "Put it all back where you found it," Vance said. "And neat like."

"Now you just don't think—!" Bill Summers began to bluster.

Vance took a stride, jammed the muzzle of the gun into the sheriff's paunch, so hard the man staggered against a wall and began to retch, clutching his middle.

"I ought to put slugs in the guts of all three of you," Vance said. "You've got no search warrant.

Legally, you've no right to enter my house. I'd be justified in doing some shooting. Now put all that stuff back, and move fast."

They were armed but they had no desire to draw. Klink and Schneer sullenly began to obey.

"You too, Summers," Vance snapped.

"You'll hear about this, Jardine," the sheriff raged, but he knew he was in the wrong and angrily began to help undo the confusion.

Their efforts were haphazard, of course, as far as neatness went, but the result was good for Vance's soul. He let them fumble around for minutes, then said, "I'll send the county the bill for the hay your horses are eating. The water is on me. Now get out. And don't come back."

"We will be back," Dolph Schneer growled as the sheriff led the posse out of the ranch yard. "That I will promise you."

"Now what do you reckon they expected to find?" Bandy asked blandly.

"A hundred thousand dollars, maybe," Vance said.

"You don't say!" Bandy exclaimed, still innocently wide-eyed. "You don't mean to say they still think you had anythin' to do with that stickup?"

"They're suspicious cusses," Vance said.

"Bein' as about twelve hundred dollars of that money belongs to you, maybe you ought to show

135

a leetle more interest in findin' out who stole it," Bandy suggested.

"Meaning that I don't act like I'm keen on running down whoever did it?"

"Well, you ain't earnin' any new friends by the way you made Bill Summers an' the rest of 'em eat crow just now. Not that the sheriff nor any o' the rest of 'em ever held any special affection for you."

In the hectic hours since the robbery, Vance had almost forgotten that he also had a financial stake in the beef money. Twelve hundred dollars would be important cash to him. It would give him a start at building up his herd again.

He saddled up and he and Bandy spent the afternoon performing the everyday chores of small ranchers. They strengthened a bog fence, doctored a cow for a gore injury, mended a head gate that irrigated the field where Bandy had a dozen acres in alfalfa.

Bandy rode into town that night, ostensibly to replenish his supply of plug tobacco, but really to keep abreast of events, and to carry out an errand for Vance.

"The sheriff an' his brave possemen air still combin' the country," he reported to Vance on his return. "Accordin' to the bulletins in the window of the *Advocate*, he expects to make an arrest soon."

The *Advocate* was the Del Rosa newspaper,

which was published once a week, but kept citizens apprised of important news in the intervals by way of bulletins pasted on its street window.

Bandy added, "All Del Rosa needs is to be embalmed an' planted. It shore died when that chunk of *dinero* went into the pocket of somebody else. Except for pot hounds, stray cats an' a goat or two, Alamo Street looked like a ghost town. I didn't see a single person dancin' in the street. An' nobody was offerin' me any free likker. Nobody."

"How about that horse you were going to look for?" Vance asked.

"Bought a seven-year-old geldin' from John Barnes at the freight corral," Bandy said. "It's a leetle swaybacked, an' with hoofs like dinner plates. Can't run a lick, but with good teeth, which means it ought to be around three, four years, at least. John agreed to deliver it to yore sister as a gift for the kids from you. He'll send it out with the first freight haul that passes by Whisky Ford. I got the bundle of clothes from Pop Rogers. The freighter will deliver that to Lisa, too."

"What did the horse cost?"

"You owe John Barnes thirty-two dollars, four bits, and a drink of whisky. I couldn't trade him down a cent under it. He first wanted fifty dollars."

"Fair enough," Vance said. "How many drinks did John give you as commission?"

Bandy ran his tongue over his lips. "John keeps a jug o' the best danged corn likker in his freight barn," he said. "I got no complaints."

After supper, Vance sat reading old newspapers and magazines by the light of the table lamp until long after normal bedtime. He kept rolling cigarettes and letting them gutter out in the cracked saucer that served as an ashtray.

He often walked out to stand in the yard, gazing at the stars. "Just to cast my weather eye around," he explained, when Bandy, who had turned in, complained. "Looks to me like we might finally have some rain. We could use it."

"We could use some sleep, too," Bandy moaned. "You an' yore weather eye! What's eatin' you? 'Tain't this hawss trader you mentioned that you're expectin', is it?"

That was the truth, but Vance didn't care to admit it. Stacy Fitzroy had said she would come to his place after dark, but, no doubt, she had decided there was nothing to discuss with him. Perhaps she had thought it over and would show up with the sheriff, and turn him and Roy Carvell over to the law. Maybe she might have decided that he and Roy had run a high blaze, and that he had been in on the holdup after all. There were a whole line of maybes that he kept running over in his mind.

He turned in at last at midnight, but still lay there a long time, sleepless. It made no difference, of course, one way or another, whether she showed up to talk the thing over with him. He had nothing to add to what she already knew. The money was gone and he did not have the least notion as to where it might be, no matter what her suspicions of him. Still, he felt somewhat cheated at her failure to appear.

As far as ranch work went the next day, it followed the routine pattern of all such days in the past. The sheriff did not return. In fact nobody came. Vance again did not fall asleep for hours that night. When he finally dozed, he had prodigious dreams.

He believed he was still dreaming and that the sound he was hearing was the thud of a jackhammer on the head of a drill in the prison quarry.

Bandy spoke, "Wake up! Somebody's knockin' on the door!"

"Vance Jardine!" Stacy Fitzroy called cautiously from outside the house. "Are you there?"

"So that one's the hawss trader? I sorta figgered it that way." Bandy sounded resigned.

Vance leaped out of the bunk. "This is a pitiful time to show up!" he snarled. "It's past midnight!"

"Are you decent?" she asked.

"You'll have to wait a minute," he growled.

"I'm usually not in the habit of going to bed with my clothes on."

"Don't light a light," she warned.

He dressed and opened the door, still stuffing in his shirt. She wore her range riding garb and a hat held by a chin-strap. A saddled horse stood in the background, tethered to the sawbuck. It smelled of warm leather and sweat.

"May I come in?" she whispered. When Vance stepped aside, she entered the dark kitchen. "It's Bandy with you, isn't it?" she asked. "I couldn't get away last night or any earlier tonight. Oak Hill is still crawling with manhunters. Bill Summers has sworn in about every able-bodied man around."

"Only the ones who'll have a vote for him at the next election," Bandy growled from the bedroom. "At a dollar a day at taxpayers' expense."

"I had to wait a chance to slip away," Stacy went on. "Juan had staked my horse out in the brush."

"Your father?" Vance asked. "How is he?"

"He's nursing a stiff neck and a headache from the sandbagging."

"He's always had the stiff neck," Bandy growled.

Stacy ignored that. "Those are nothing to other things. He blames himself for the robbery. He feels he failed the men in the pool."

"How does he explain the junk in those boxes in place of the money?" Vance demanded.

"He doesn't know."

"What do you mean, he doesn't know?"

She bristled. "Of course he doesn't. He thinks the money was still in the boxes."

"And you didn't tell him any different?"

"I did not. That would really crush him."

"But, if your father didn't steal that money and fill the boxes with scrap iron, then who did?"

"That's what I want to find out. It was done before they reached Oak Hill. I'm convinced of that. The exchange must have been made somewhere on the way from Platte City."

Bandy again took a hand. "You don't mean the major was stupid enough to let them boxes o' cash lie around loose with nobody lookin' out to see that somebody didn't slip in a bunch of junk?"

She remained silent. "Is that what happened?" Vance asked. "Were they careless? Is that what you're trying to make us believe?"

"I'm not trying to make you believe anything. All I want is to take a good look at those boxes. I was so upset the other night I didn't really examine them closely."

"You may have a point," Vance admitted. "I've had some such idea in mind myself."

"Where are they?"

"Buried. In the barn at the Carvell place. In the box stall. All the junk is still in them."

She left the house at a run, heading for her horse. Vance overtook her, seizing her by the arm, halting her. "You're not going over there tonight to try to dig those things up?"

"I certainly am."

"At this hour? You're loco!"

"Well, you wouldn't want me to try it in daylight, would you. Someone might see me and become inquisitive. You really wouldn't care to have that happen, now would you? For the sake of your brother-in-law, at least."

"All right," he raged. "I'll go with you. You knew you could badger me into it when you came here. Let's hope, for the sake of your father's infernal pride, that none of Bill Summers's posse happen to spot us."

He buckled on his six-shooter, caught up his horse and saddled. Without a word, they rode away. Bandy stood in the dark doorway, obviously disapproving of all that was going on.

Reaching Hat Creek, they left the horses at a distance. Vance moved to the house and tapped lightly on the door until his sister responded. Roy Carvell was in the house, awake.

"We're going to take a look at the express boxes, Lisa," Vance whispered. "Maybe we might learn something. Go back to bed."

"Who's with you?" Roy called from an inner room.

"Never mind that," Vance replied. "Did Bill Summers show up?"

"Yes," Roy answered. "Him an' a couple others, but they went away without more'n sniffin' around an' askin' a few questions. They mainly only wanted to know if we'd sighted any suspicious persons lately."

Vance borrowed the unlighted kitchen lamp. "Johnny Barnes will send out a horse that's safe for Fern and Chad to ride," he told Lisa. "It's a birthday present from Bandy and me, along with a few other things the freighter will deliver."

He added as a parting shot at his brother-in-law, "It's a thirty-dollar horse, Roy, but keep your hands off it. Its ownership is in Chad and Fern's name, with their mother as trustee. If I hear of you trying to sell it for whisky money I'll build a fire under your tail a mile long."

He and Stacy went to the barn. He lighted the lamp, found the shovel and soon had the three boxes excavated. He dragged them out of the stall, located a wagon tarp which he spread and on which he upended the contents.

He and Stacy delved through the jumble of rusty metal and stones. Vance singled out two bars of lead, each weighing about four pounds.

"Galena lead," he observed. "At least these things are worth a few dollars apiece. They go

143

back to the days when buffalo hunters molded their own slugs for their .50 Sharps. Fact is, lots of hunters still do. Galena lead still costs good money. Whoever fixed up these boxes must have wanted to make sure the weight came out the same as the gold so that the major wouldn't become suspicious. They had to use whatever was heavy and compact and handy, and they didn't hold back at wasting a little money to earn a lot more."

Stacy peered at him, a frown pinching at the bridge of her nose. "Are you trying to tell me something?" she asked.

"I'd say that whoever worked this sleight-of-hand didn't do it on a minute's notice," Vance said. "He—or they—were able to take their time, fixing up these substitute boxes. They must even have had scales handy to weigh them."

She stared at him excitedly. "*Substitute* boxes? Why, of course! It had to be that way. Nobody could have merely taken out the money and replaced it with this trash. That would have taken too long, been too awkward to accomplish. I see your point. This thing was well planned in advance. But where?"

He picked up a railroad spike. It was rusty and had seen long use, for its head had been battered by mallets. There were several other damaged spikes in the heap.

"A lot of this is old railroad iron," he said.

144

He scrabbled through the heap, and singled out a short, flanged length of broken metal. It was pierced by sizable holes.

He moved nearer the lamp, turning the object over and over, peering. "Now, maybe we're getting somewhere!" he exclaimed.

"What is it?" Stacy asked.

"This is what railroad men call a chair," Vance said. "It's sort of an iron cradle they place under the rails, to which they spike both the chair and the rail to the ties. These holes are for spikes. Some railroads use things called fishplates to join the rails together."

"Where did you pick up such knowledge?" Stacy asked without interest.

"In the prison rock quarry. I helped lay more than one stretch of railroad spur in the quarry. A couple of the cons were old-time railroad section hands who'd worked all over the country. One of them had helped spike rails on the Union Pacific, and was at Promontory Point the day the transcontinental line was finished. Take a look at this."

Stacy moved close and voiced aloud the letters that were faintly visible, molded into the surface of the length of railroad scrap iron. "RIC." She looked at him, puzzled. "RIC," she repeated. "What does it mean?"

"Reading Iron Company," Vance said. "Reading, Pennsylvania."

"Stop being so mysterious, and tell me what this means!"

"I remember this old-timer saying that most of the original Union Pacific track equipment was made by the Reading Iron Company."

She didn't grasp the significance of it for a moment. Then she became excited.

Vance nodded. "The likeliest place to find one of the old-style Union Pacific rail chairs would be on or near the Union Pacific Railroad. And that would be a long way from Texas. A thousand miles or so. A place about as far away as this Platte City, for instance. We all know the U.P. runs through Platte City, for that's where your father sold the Del Rosa herd."

She clapped her hands and laughed wildly. "Now you'll believe!" she cried.

"Believe what?"

"That my father was cheated right at the start. It's my belief now that he never had the gold in his possession. Somehow, through some trickery, these fake treasure chests were palmed off on him at Platte City. They were never opened. The seals were still intact when your brother-in-law and his ruffian pals stole the boxes at Oak Hill."

Vance had a new thought. He began examining the three empty express boxes. They had seen long service and bore the scars of rough handling and rough weather over the years. Their sides were worn and tarnished by jostling in the boots of countless stagecoaches.

Vance discarded one, then a second. The third box was far from new, but it had seen considerably less service than the others. Vance went over it inch by inch. He finally carried it outside to the horse trough and used water, rubbing vigorously on the wooden surface. He returned, and he and Stacy peered in the lamplight at the result. Dim, but legible, they could make out the words that had been countersunk in small letters in the bottom of the box.

PROPERTY OF
WELLS FARGO & CO.,
BUFFALO BEND DIV.
WYOMING.

"I never heard of Buffalo Bend," Vance ruminated. "And Wyoming covers a lot of territory, so I've been told."

"I never heard of it either, but it won't be hard to find out just where it is," Stacy said. "One thing is sure. It's up there, and I'll bet you a tin dime it's not far from Platte City. These boxes came from that stage line. It only helps prove my father is innocent."

"I'm not saying the major is entirely in the clear in my mind, even though you are very convincing," Vance said. "But, if he really was bamboozled up in that country, he can kiss that hundred thousand dollars a sad goodby."

Her lips drooped. "You are probably right," she sighed. "And you can kiss ten or eleven thousand dollars goodby also."

"Ten or eleven *thousand?*"

"I know Bandy slipped more than forty head of your 7-11s into the beef drive. That, along with the reward, would add up to about eleven thousand dollars, I'm sure."

"Reward?"

"You don't seem to have kept up with the news. My father is offering ten percent of any of the stolen money to whoever recovers it. That would amount to about ten thousand dollars. He intends to pay it out of his own share. A man with eleven thousand dollars to spend, and a little get-up about him, could take over half a dozen of these little outfits around here," she said. "He could be rich in a few years. Beef is coming back. My father is sure of it, and he's never been wrong yet when it comes to things like that. You know the value of grading up a herd."

Vance eyed her, surprised. "Who'd ever have thought that Anastasia Fitzroy had anything as solid as that inside her head."

"Anastasia Fitzroy's head isn't quite as solid as the head of someone I could mention. And if you call me by that infernal name again, I'll slap you. At least I didn't throw away two years of my life for nothing."

"I don't know what you're talking about."

"Oh, yes you do. I heard enough the other day when you were laying down the law to Roy Carvell to know—"

"You know nothing. Do you understand that?"

She spoke soberly. "I was wrong when I said you did it for nothing. It was for Lisa and the children. I understand that. It may have been worth it. I'm not the one to say, one way or the other."

"You're not to say anything."

"Someone has to go to this Platte City and find out who stole that money," she said.

"You've heard that old saw about the needle and the haystack, haven't you?" Vance jeered. "That money's probably a thousand miles from this Platte City by this time."

"Perhaps. But to find it you will have to start looking for it at Platte City."

"*Who* will have to start there?"

"You, Mister Smarty Jardine."

"Me? Oh, no you don't. I—"

"Who else? Doesn't the chance to earn eleven thousand dollars mean anything to you? Think what it would do, not only for you but for Lisa and the children."

"You're really driving the spurs deep, aren't you? I tell you that money is scattered over half the West by this time. It's been three weeks at least since—"

"I doubt if it's scattered," she said. "In fact I've reason to believe it probably is still hidden somewhere in or around Platte City, and will remain there for a long time."

"You're dreaming. Maybe that's where you got such an idea. Wake up!"

"My father says the money was in newly minted twenty-dollar goldpieces, dated this present year. A bank at Platte City handled the arrangements. The herd was sold to the buyer of a big meat-packing company at Chicago. The money was drawn on a Chicago bank, and my father asked that it be paid in gold, knowing that people down here still aren't too sure about Yankee greenbacks being worth face value. The gold was shipped by train in Wells Fargo boxes. My father counted it in the presence of the banker and men from the crew, and it was put back in the express boxes, locked and sealed."

"And so—?"

"Those double-eagles bore no mint mark, which meant that it had been coined at the Philadelphia mint. The banker at Platte City said it had been the first double-eagle mint of the year that he had seen."

"Once more I begin to see what's working in that head of yours," Vance said. "The next thing to do is—"

"I've already done it. I rode into town and talked to Cal Fairbanks at the *Advocate*. Cal acts as news correspondent for the *San Antonio Light*, and for the Associated Press. I told him about the stolen money being newly minted, and that everyone should start watching for it to appear and report it to the sheriff. Cal gets space rates for news stories. He telegraphed it immediately to the San Antonio paper and the Associated Press. He's also getting out a special edition of the *Advocate* to notify people around here to be on the look-out."

"You seem to have figured this whole thing out before you cost me a night's sleep and bamboozled me into pawing through this stuff," Vance growled.

"I went over it all with my father, step by step. I became convinced the money had been substituted right at the start at Platte City, but it was only a guess. This confirms it."

"Did you tell Cal Fairbanks the truth about what was in the express boxes?"

"Of course not. He believes, like everyone else, the money was stolen at Oak Hill. However, the news story about the coins being easy to identify will surely get to Platte City. That ought to be enough to make whoever has them to lie mighty low for quite a spell, at least until twenty-dollar goldpieces of this year's Philadelphia mintage become common."

"I can't see one person as having swung this thing," Vance commented. "Whoever did it had to have help. Exactly what made you so sure the trick was pulled at Platte City?"

"There didn't seem to be any other explanation. Dad said the express boxes were never out of sight of them all the way to Oak Hill. There were always at least two men from the pool on guard over it. Dad says he stayed with the boxes personally the biggest part of the time, and even slept with the ugly things several times."

Vance rubbed his jaw thoughtfully. He absently reflected that he needed a shave. "Damned whiskers never quit growing," he ruminated. "And I've got to hone my razor."

"Now who cares a hoot about—"

"I was just thinking," Vance admitted. He made a sudden decision. "I'll talk to the major."

"Then you *are* going?" she cried elatedly. "To Platte City? You're really going there?"

"All I said was I'd talk to the major. There might have been a time somehow, somewhere along the line when the boxes were traded, maybe right under his eyes. I want to go over it with him. When?"

"Well, it can't be while the sheriff and his men are around. If Bill Summers saw you at Oak Hill, he'd want to know why. We'll have to wait until tonight. Come to the ranch after dark. Stop at the windmill north of the pasture. I'll meet you there if the coast is clear. Say nine o'clock. If I don't show up, I'll get in touch with you later, somehow."

For lack of a better hiding place, they restored the contents of the three boxes and buried them again in the box stall.

"I'll be at the windmill tonight," Vance told her, "if the major will talk to me. He never went out of his way to take notice of anyone named Jardine in the past."

"That was because your father was so blasted high and mighty!" she burst out.

"What's that? *My* father? High and mighty? Now, you're twisting things around again. It's been the Fitzroys who've always acted like it hurt their eyes even to see a Jardine in the distance."

"Who was it that everybody admired and wanted to be seen with?" she demanded. "Who was the dashing, chance-taking gambler, the idol of all the young cowhands in the Del Rosa? Who was it who'd been decorated by General Lee for bravery in the war? Who was it that strutted and swaggered?"

She was suddenly almost sobbing. "Who was it who ran away with the girl my father had hoped to marry?"

"You know about that?" Vance asked, shocked.

"Blast you, Vance Jardine, you've always had the best of it!"

"The *best* of it?"

"You were always so independent, so carefree. You were the one they wanted to imitate, just as they did your father. They didn't even hold it against you when you were sent to prison. They put it down as just a prank. Then you had to come home a hero, just like your father."

"You must be talking about someone else," Vance protested.

"And you had love and affection in your home. There were no memories, no bitterness, no sitting at a table with a father who had only pride to live for, and with a mother who would always believe she had been second choice."

Weeping, she ran to her horse and mounted. "Tonight!" she choked. "Be there."

She rode away. Vance had meant to tell her that he wasn't making any promises but he did not speak. He was almost appalled by the glimpse she had given him of the true state of things at Oak Hill, whose lord and ladies had been so envied all these years by the people of the Del Rosa.

10

Once more it was nearing daybreak when Vance unsaddled at his ranch. Bandy pretended to remain asleep as he turned in. Bandy still asked no questions when he awakened early in the afternoon and ate what amounted to a combined breakfast and dinner.

"I'm going on a little ride tonight," he finally told Bandy. "I'm going to write out a will."

"A will is a mighty smart thing to write fer a feller who rides at night as much as you've been doin' lately," Bandy commented.

"There's a chance I might not be back for a spell, this time," Vance said.

"That means you think there's a chance you might never come back," Bandy said quietly. "I'd say you might be gittin' the worst o' this hawss trade. Yore life is a purty big price to offer. Nothin' comes any higher."

"The ranch is yours if anything should happen to me," Vance said. "It's going to be half yours anyway, even if I do come back."

"The more you talk the less I like it," Bandy said. "Is somebody gunnin' fer you?"

"Not yet, but it might come up that way."

"Would it do any good if I came along?"

"It's a one-man job," Vance said. "And I don't

know for sure just where I'm going, or how to get there."

He made out a brief will, placed it in a drawer and rolled another cigarette. "Don't judge people by the starch in their collars," he said after a long period during which he honed his razor and shaved meticulously. "Not even the Fitzroys."

"The Fitzroys? Them snobbish—?"

"Even snobs have their grief. It makes it worse when they're too proud to show it and keep it bottled up inside 'em for years and years."

Bandy didn't understand and still didn't understand when Vance shook hands with him and rode away shortly after dark. The night was warm and humid. Sheet lightning played in the Armadillo Hills to the west, but the storm rolled northward. The wind brought the cooling freshness of rain that had fallen somewhere.

The stars dimmed a trifle in the mist of the scattering storm. An armadillo went lumbering and rattling out of his way. Bats circled overhead as he crossed Latigo Creek and he heard javelinas grunting in the thickets.

The lights of the Fitzroy ranch appeared far ahead, beaded among the ancient oaks that crowned the crest of a rise. He dismounted near a windmill whose vanes were set to catch the irregular breeze, and whose clanking labors brought small spurts of water into the tank. In the darkness he was aware of the nearby presence of cattle, but they were bedded and content for the night. Crickets were united in their ceaseless concert that was like the beat of a pulse in the balmy night.

He waited, longing for the solace of a smoke, but refraining for fear it would bring someone to investigate.

Then Stacy came out of the starlight. She was on foot. She wore skirts and a blouse and had a lace *rebosa* over her hair in the Mexican style.

"It's all right," she murmured. "Leave your horse here."

She led the way, circling well clear of the bunkhouse where lamps burned and from which came the occasional sound of men's voices. The ruins of the stock shed gave forth the musty, dank odor of soaked, charred timber.

They entered the main house by a side door. This opened into a hall which was dimly illuminated by lamplight from the open door of a side room. Stacy moved to this door, motioning him to follow. It was a sizable bedroom. Stacy's mother sat in a rocking chair, a book in her hand from which she had been reading aloud.

Her husband, in an easy chair, his feet, in slippers, propped on a hassock, had been listening—or pretending, Vance surmised. His wife, palpably, had been trying to divert and soothe the troubled mind of her husband. In the past, Major Webster Fitzroy had always taken proper care of his figure, and was fastidious of dress. He now wore a dressing gown over a nightshirt. He was unshaven and haggard. A whisky bottle and a glass stood on a stand at his side.

He came to his feet, staring disbelievingly at Vance. "What are you doing in this house, Jardine?" he roared.

"I'm not sure myself," Vance said. "It's the first time I've ever been asked to step across the doorstep of this place."

"I brought Mr. Jardine here," Stacy said. "Mother, I am sure you have met him."

Her mother laid aside the book. "Of course," she said. "I've known him since he was a baby. I knew his lovely mother."

She offered her hand. Vance walked to her, took her hand. Then he did something he had never done in his life, nor ever thought of doing. He leaned and kissed the hand of this handsome, gray-eyed, composed person. He was seeing in Amanda Fitzroy the strength and character of a woman who had refused to turn bitter, who had remained faithful to her marriage vows and had been the strong staff on which Web Fitzroy had leaned.

"You take after your mother," Amanda Fitzroy said. "You have her eyes, her mouth. But there's much of your father in you, too. Ah, but he was a gay, handsome man."

Vance's throat was tight. Anything he might have said would only have hurt everyone who was listening. It was Web Fitzroy who remained true to the stern image he had built up. "Get out of this house, Jardine. I'll have none of your kind here."

"He came here to talk to you, Dad," Stacy said.

"About what?"

"I want him to listen while we go over again everything you remember about the express boxes," she said. "Every minute of the time you spent in Platte City, every moment of the trip to Oak Hill."

Web Fitzroy became purple with offended pride. "Why should I waste my time? I've already gone over—"

"It's important," his daughter said. "Believe it, Dad, it might be the most important thing in your life."

Vance spoke. "In the first place, just where *is* this Platte City?"

Web Fitzroy fought for control of his temper. "It's west of Julesburg, as any educated person should know," he fumed. "On the Union Pacific Railroad."

"And a place called Buffalo Bend?" Vance questioned.

"I never heard of—" the major began. Then he paused, and added, "On second thought I believe

I did hear of some such a town, but it can't amount to much."

"Let's go over it, little by little," Vance urged. "Just how and when was the beef money turned over to you?"

"What sort of an inquisition is this?" Web Fitzroy raged. "Are you trying to usurp Sheriff Summers's duties? Stacy, why did you try to humiliate me by bringing this scoundrel here?"

"Your daughter is doing her best to find that money in order to spare you a lot of trouble," Vance said. "I understand that you've offered a reward of ten percent of any that is recovered."

"That is so," Web Fitzroy thundered. "But—"

"And no questions asked?"

"No! By all that's holy, I won't agree to any such—"

His daughter cut him off. "And no question asked," she said. "Father, that provision is not to spare the guilty, but to avoid disgrace for innocent persons, perhaps."

"So that's it!" her father raged. "Then you *did* have a hand in the robbery, Jardine, and you now have the effrontery to try to make a profit out of it and escape the penalty for the crime. I knew you were in it right from the start."

"No, Dad," his daughter protested. "He's doing this only at my request."

"I'll send you back to prison where you came from," her father rasped, ignoring her. "Where is the money your pals took from this house?"

"We feel that question can be answered at Platte City, Father," Stacy said.

"I don't understand."

"That is all we can tell you," she said. "Please believe me when I say that we are doing the best we know to find the money."

He turned furiously on Vance. "I *demand* that you tell me who the scoundrels were who slugged me and—!"

"And saved you from being looked on as a bigger fool than you already are," Vance said.

Web Fitzroy looked at his daughter. "You haven't turned against me, darling?" he said hollowly. "Not you?"

His wife came to his side. "Of course not, Webster," she said and drew his head against her. "She loves you." She added gently, "And so do I."

"Don't pity me," he said brokenly. "I don't deserve pity. It is the worst that could happen to me."

Vance looked at Stacy and led the way out of the room. Her eyes were swimming. "It's no use," he said. "He won't tell me anything. It probably wouldn't do any good anyway. If the money was substituted between here and Platte City, he doesn't know when or where."

She motioned him into another room which opened off the hall. It turned out to be her bedroom. It was spacious, with chintz-covered chairs. A brass-bowl lamp with a globular shade was lighted, the wick turned low. An unfinished dress lay on a sewing table.

She drew up a chair for him, but he preferred to stand. "How soon can you start?" she said.

He glared. "You're taking it for granted that I'm going to try to find this needle."

When she did not speak, he added testily, "Exactly why me?"

"If you were doing the choosing, who in this range would you pick? A bumblefoot like the sheriff? A blatherskite like any of half dozen others I could name? A weakling like your brother-in-law?"

She waited. When Vance failed to come up with an adequate retort, she went on, "There are several points against you, of course. For one thing, I don't believe you care about the reward. You won't really have your heart set on it. Also, you are reckless, and too quick to flare up if you think anyone is trying to patronize you. You're vain and conceited."

"Ho!" Vance jeered. "Conceited, am I? The Fitzroys have had a corner on all that sort of thing ever since I can remember."

"On the other hand," she continued, "you are fairly intelligent. I believe, also, that you've seen enough of the rough side of life and have been in prison in contact with men of the criminal type

162

so that you should be able to cope with them and to look at things from their viewpoint. You have also managed to lose a lot of that drawl that might mark you as from this part of Texas. I happen to know that you can take care of yourself in case of trouble."

"I doubt if that's supposed to be flattery."

"In a way, perhaps. You used to be the toughest kid in school when it came to defending yourself. You dealt out black eyes without fear or favor. You apparently are still handy with your fists. You've been home only a few days and you've already slugged two citizens in the jaw, not to mention roughing up your brother-in-law."

"We're getting off the subject. You were mentioning the possibility there might be trouble connected with this affair you're trying to crowd me into."

"You know that as well as I do. Whoever planned this must be intelligent, and has proved he, or they, will not stop at murder. Remember, they've already tried to kill Roy Carvell."

"Anastasia," Vance said, "you've persuaded me to stay out of it. I don't hanker to get myself rubbed out."

"I'll see you in jail," she said sweetly.

"That," he remarked, "did not sound very nice."

"I could go to the sheriff and mention that you buried three Wells Fargo express boxes in

163

your brother-in-law's barn. Also that this same brother-in-law had a bullet in him. It might take the two of you a long time to explain all this. Maybe even years. In Huntsville."

"You wouldn't do it, of course."

"Are you sure?" She was innocently wide-eyed.

"It isn't in you, but you'd make a mighty good poker player, as well as a smart horse trader. You know when to push your luck."

"I know how to call a four-flush," she said. "And you were four-flushing when you acted like you wanted to back out. Let's quit jabbing at each other. I need your help. You need mine. You certainly could use that reward money. I don't want to see us lose Oak Hill."

"Speaking of poker, I'd better head for town," Vance said. "I might be able to sit in a game for a couple of hours before closing time."

"Whatever for?"

"It'll cost a little money to get to this Platte City," he explained. "I can't quite swing it with what I've got in my wallet. I might win a pot or two."

She glared at him. "Of all the contemptible, cantankerous humans!" she said grimly. "You've known all the time you were going, and you've just been stringing me along."

"Yes, ma'am," Vance said meekly. "I always sort of liked to get you tempered up."

"I should have known better than to have asked you to get into this," she said. "But, as for money, I've already taken care of that."

She delved into a drawer and produced a purse from which she counted gold coins. "Three hundred dollars," she said. "That ought to be enough to get you to Platte City. I'll see that you get more if it's needed. It's my own money."

His expression annoyed her. "It's no insult to accept expense money in a case like this, even from a female. You've no time to worry about your scruples. And even less to waste trying to win at poker. The quicker you get to Platte City the better. Besides, even *you,* might lose."

"What kind of a dig is that?" he demanded.

"I've heard that wise men have learned not to play poker with the likes of you."

He eyed her stormily. "If that's so, has it occurred to you that something might happen to that hundred thousand dollars if the likes of me got my hands on it?"

"We'll ford that river when we come to it."

"What you're saying is that you believe in sending a crook to catch a crook."

"You're still wasting time," she said. "You must start at once. Tonight."

"Tonight? Isn't that being a little sudden?"

"I'll loan you a good saddle horse to get you to Sandoval. You can take the stage there the rest of the way to San Antonio. Leave the horse at the livery in Sandoval. You will go by train, of course, from San Antonio to Platte City. That will take about a week, but it's the fastest way. Here's a written schedule of the best route. It was the one by which my father and the others came from Platte City."

She thrust a paper into his hand. "You sort of keep two jumps ahead of me, don't you?" he complained.

"I doubt it. I rather think you came prepared to leave tonight. You know the value of wasted time as well as I do."

"All I know is I got no other clothes to wear."

"You can buy what you need in San Antonio. I'll get word to Bandy Plunkett that you will be away for a while."

"Don't bother. I told Bandy I might be gone for a spell."

"Just as I suspected. You knew when you came here that—"

"I had a hunch I'd be bludgeoned into it whether I wanted in or not," he said. "I was right."

She smiled a little. "I'll warn Bandy not to talk. It's better that no one in Del Rosa knows you're on your way to Platte City. That's why it's best to take the stage at Sandoval rather than boarding it in town. You're not known in that country up there, and—"

She paused, stricken by a sudden thought. "At least I hope you're not. I've been taking it for granted you've never been in this Platte City."

"We're safe on that score," he said. "Haven't been within five hundred miles of it. If anybody happens to be on the stage to San'tone who knows me I'll tell him I'm going there to play a little poker. Most folks would believe that."

She looked at the six-shooter he was carrying. She delved into a drawer and produced a wicked-looking, double-barreled derringer which she handed him. "That's for insurance," she said. "It's one of a brace that belongs to Mother. She gave me this one after that affair at the ranch the other night."

"Your mother? She packs a derringer?"

"Not usually. She really prefers to use a horsewhip. Here are a few extra cartridges. Fifty caliber. I doubt if you'll use them. There's a saying about these nasty little guns. You might only need one once in your life, but when you do, you will need it mighty bad."

"And there's an old saying in the Jardine family," he replied. "Never look a pistol in the muzzle, especially when it's a sneak gun, to which I never was partial. I'm getting a feeling you know more about what I might be getting into than you let on. Have you already got my measurements for a coffin?"

Again she was very sober. "Not exactly. But, you know as well as I that there could be danger. I have told you everything I know. I've learned a few details about Platte City in talking to my father that might be of help to you."

She recounted the information. Platte City was much larger than Del Rosa—perhaps triple its size. In addition to being a railroad division point it was the business center and shipping place for ranches over a wide area as well as the crossroads for wagon freighting and feeder stagecoach lines.

"Twenty gambling houses and not a church is the way Father described it," she added. "It sounds like an ideal place for you. Gambling houses and saloons are where a person with keen ears might pick up some information.

"You'll have to play some poker, no doubt, as an excuse for being around those places. I would advise you not to be too—shall we say—lucky, at it. People might be more likely to talk to a person they considered about their equal."

"You mean I'm to be a tinhorn?"

"Exactly. I will furnish you with a little more money from time to time, but my finances are not what you might call inexhaustible. So be moderate in your gambling."

"Say now," Vance said, brightening. "I never before had a chance to draw on somebody else's bankroll when I wanted to try to fill an inside straight. This looks like one game at which I can't lose."

"You can lose," she said grimly. "And more

168

than money, if you're not careful. You'll adopt another name, of course. After all, someone up there might have heard of Vance Jardine, the hero of Huntsville Penitentiary. What name will you prefer?"

"I haven't given it a thought. I bet you have."

"I believe something like, say Lance Harding, would do. It sounds close enough to Vance Jardine to be about right."

"I was right. You *had* given it some thought."

She beckoned him to follow and led him out of the house. In a secluded spot stood one of the big, lean-haunched saddle animals her father had developed. Vance's rigging had been transferred to this animal.

"There's no end to your efficiency," Vance said. "I don't have to do any thinking for myself, do I?"

"I'm sure you will find that necessary," she said. She held out a very cool, very formal hand. "Good night! And good luck. Don't try to write me until you hear from me. Any mail bearing a Platte City postmark might arouse suspicion in Del Rosa."

"You mean you can't trust your neighbors?"

"Good night," she said again.

She stood there as Vance mounted and rode away. He was considerably let-down by the matter-of-fact way in which she had sent him on this mission.

11

It was a week later when Vance made connection with a westbound Union Pacific express at the raw prairie town of Grand Island, Nebraska. He climbed wearily aboard. It had been a week of uncertainty, of wondering why he had let himself become involved in so fragile a quest—a week of frustration, of changing trains, of long waits in dreary railway stations at junctions he never wanted to see again.

He had been on the point of turning back many times, and was again debating the decision as he walked through the train, following a porter who carried his lone suitcase. The cars were Pullmans, for this was a new, crack train that the railroad had placed in operation. It sported a dining car ahead, and at the rear was a gleaming palace car with an open observation platform.

The day was ghastly hot, and the passengers were slumped in leather seats, fanning themselves, wrung limp. The train got under way, and more miles of buffalo grass prairie unreeled, broken by the soddies and tarpaper shacks of homesteaders.

Vance left his piece of luggage in the section to which he was led, then headed rearward for the observation car. Passing down the length of one of the Pullmans, he halted in stride as though he had encountered an invisible barrier. He stood balancing himself as the train picked up speed. Then he stepped back a pace and took a second look at two feminine travelers who occupied one of the seats.

"Tell me it can't be true!" he moaned, stunned.

"If you are trying to annoy us, sir," Stacy Fitzroy said primly, "I'll call the conductor. We do not wish the attentions of strangers."

Vance took the hint and moved on. Stacy was accompanied by her mother. They wore cheap, ruffled cotton blouses with puffed sleeves, and striped skirts, and buttoned shoes. They had on straw bonnets equipped with veils to protect them from the grime of travel. Corkscrew curls hung from beneath the brim of Stacy's bonnet. A suitcase of the same imitation leather quality as his own, along with two carpetbags, crowded their section.

He moved on through the palace car to the open observation platform. There were chairs, but at the moment the platform was unoccupied, except for himself. It was noisy, hot and dusty.

The palace car was a new luxury in transcontinental travel, but few ladies took advantage of it, for among its benefits was a well-stocked bar where alcoholic spirits were served. It was the gathering place for boisterous males and fast females.

However, glancing over his shoulder, he soon saw Stacy picking her way modestly past the convivial passengers. She came to the open platform. She pretended to be interested only in the scenery, keeping her back turned to him as she spoke.

"We've had the devil's own time catching up with you," she complained. "You didn't follow the route I laid out for you. We got aboard this train a day ago at Council Bluffs. You seem to have come by some other way."

"I did," Vance snarled. "What in the blue flames are you two doing here?"

"Three pairs of ears will have a much better chance of learning something at Platte City than one pair," she said. "Mother is a poor widow woman, bound west to start a new life, along with other immigrants. I am her daughter, hoping to find a husband."

Vance eyed her, being particularly offended by the corkscrew curls and the yellow, buttoned shoes that glared from beneath the hem of her skirt. "I wish you luck," he said. "It would take a brave man. The curls? Strike me blind!"

"They're false," she said complacently. "I bought them in San Antonio, along with the rest of our wardrobes." She turned and gave Vance a brief, searching inspection. "I can't say you're exactly a picture of elegance," she commented. "You're a sorry imitation of a tinhorn gambler.

One-dollar straw hat, rainbow silk vest, second-hand plantation coat that's been slept in, celluloid collar and rather grimy ruffled shirt with string tie."

"Thank you," Vance said. "That's exactly the effect I wanted. It set me back eighteen dollars and fifty cents in San Antonio. Your money."

"You apparently shopped at the same second-hand store where Mother and I outfitted," she said.

"Exactly what are your plans when you reach Platte City?" Vance asked caustically. "Or have you given them any thought?"

"I'll try to catch on as a clerk in some enterprise that is patronized by the public where I can listen to conversations. Mother hasn't decided what she will do."

"There are always the music halls," Vance said. "Would they be public enough for your purpose?"

"That," she said with sugary calm, "will be only as a last resort. I'll keep your suggestion in mind. However, I'm sure you can take care of all the eavesdropping in such places—and feel right at home. I'll try somewhere else."

"I might have expected some such stunt as this from you, but I didn't count on your mother being rattle-brained too."

"I had planned on coming alone, but she insisted that I needed protection," she said.

She added, "Mother's name, by the way, is now Mrs. Jenny Royce. I am Miss Stella Royce, her daughter, young, vivacious, unmarried and not above flirting with the right person, especially if I believe I can learn anything of value from him."

"I'll do my best to avoid you," Vance said devoutly. "You spell trouble. So does your mother."

"I'm afraid you are right," she said. "I would advise you to get off this train at the next stop and go back. That is why we have been so anxious to overtake you. Get out of this whole mess." The lightness was gone from her voice.

"Something's happened," Vance said. "What is it?"

She hesitated an instant. "Your brother-in-law is dead," she said.

"Roy? Roy Carvell?"

"He went to the barn the morning after you left Oak Hill to take care of his horse," she said. "When he didn't come back, Lisa found him lying there. He'd been hit with something. His skull was crushed."

Vance was silent for a space, chilled. "Someone came back to make sure he was dead and wouldn't talk," he said. "Len Kelso?"

"Bill Summers questioned Len, not that he really suspected him, but only that Len and Roy Carvell had been friends, and Len might have some information. Len had nothing that would help, but he *did* have a perfect alibi. He had been in Del Rosa that night, drinking and playing cards, and had bunked at the hotel."

"Sam Jones, then," Vance said. "Who ever he is. At least Len and this Sam Jones didn't head for Mexico as Roy believed. Didn't it occur to Bill Summers that Roy's murder might be tied in with the holdup at Oak Hill?"

"Even he might have had some such thought. If so, nothing came of it. He finally decided that Roy must have been kicked by his horse. I didn't see any point in setting him straight. Not at that time, at least. It would only have warned this Sam Jones to be on guard. It proves one thing. The people we're dealing with have no qualms about committing murder to protect themselves. Go home. Money isn't worth risking your life for."

"How about you and your mother? What are *your* lives worth?"

"We're wasting time discussing it."

"You two are still going ahead with it? Going to Platte City?"

"We're women. In the first place, they'd never suspect us. In the second place, they'd surely not harm women."

"I doubt both theories," Vance said. "I doubt them very strongly. As the hero of Huntsville Penitentiary, I'd never be able to look at myself

175

again in a shaving mirror if I let two misguided females go there to face the dragon alone. In addition to my brother-in-law cashing in, did anything else happen before you left home that might throw light on this matter?"

"Yes," she began. But other passengers, slightly inebriated, came pouring noisily out of the car onto the platform, carrying glasses and goblets. "I'll tell you at first chance after we get to Platte City," she whispered hurriedly.

"I'm not getting off at Platte City," Vance said. "I'm going on to Buffalo Bend. Do you remember that name?"

"Of course. But why, for pity's sake?"

"Mainly because 'they,' whoever they are, will likely be expecting somebody from Del Rosa to show up in Platte City most any day now. If I were they, I'd be keeping an eye on persons getting off express trains from the east. I figure I'd attract less attention arriving from Buffalo Bend on a local train from the west, or even by saddleback or stagecoach. This Buffalo Bend is only about an hour's ride by train beyond Platte City, according to the schedule."

He added, "In addition, I'm curious about those three express boxes. Remember, they were owned by a stagecoach division that seems to operate out of this Buffalo Bend. It might pay to take a look there first."

"You may be right," she agreed. She pushed

through the boisterous group and made her way into the palace car, and vanished toward her section ahead. She left Vance frustrated, with many questions on his tongue. He had one solace, at least. Since the night she had so casually shaken hands with him after drawing from him the promise that he would go to Platte City, he had been nursing an injured memory of that abrupt parting. He realized now that, in her viewpoint, it had not been a parting at all— only a brief intermission. He suddenly felt much lighter in spirit.

He had a train schedule in his pocket which told him that the express would be due in Platte City at eight o'clock the next evening. Buffalo Bend was listed as a flag stop, which meant that trains such as these paused there only when there were passengers to board or depart.

During the remainder of the journey, he avoided Stacy and her mother, spending his time between sleeping hours, mainly in the palace car.

As sundown of the next day came, his watch told him the train was running more than an hour late. He waited with some curiosity as the train pulled into the station at Platte City. As Stacy had told him, the town was of some size and importance. There was the usual quota of idlers on the platform, and the customary scurry of citizens who had come there to meet arrivals or see passengers off.

Amid that confusion it was impossible to say whether there was any particular person on the platform who was giving more than ordinary attention to arrivals. He sank back in his seat, a trifle let-down, as the train got under way again, and pushed ahead into the darkness of the open plain.

The conductor, who was more than normally huffy, found him presently and warned him that Buffalo Bend was the next stop, and to be ready instantly to depart.

"The next time I see that ticket butcher at Grand Island what booked you to this flag stop, I'll punch him in the nose," the conductor growled as he ordered a vestibule opened for Vance's departure. "This'll cost us another five minutes or more, an' we're runnin' way late already."

The man added, "As long as we're stoppin' there, anyway, two fool women in the car ahead, have bought fare on to the Bend too, instead o' gettin' off at Platte City an' waitin' fer the local. It saved them some trouble, at least."

"Two women?"

He had no chance to pursue the subject, for the conductor had hurried away. The train jolted to a stop and a porter practically pushed him down the steps and handed him his suitcase.

The train barely paused, resuming its way with a great puffing and clatter. The lights of the parlor car slid past and dwindled westward. Vance peered at two feminine figures that stood huddled together in the darkness, their baggage lying beside them on the gravel.

He picked up his suitcase. Its major weight was the six-shooter, belt and holster, and the derringer which he had stored there along with a shaving kit and a few articles of spare clothing that he had bought at San Antonio.

Stacy and her mother came with a rush to join him and pushed close to his side as they gazed apprehensively around. A vast dome of stars blazed overhead. Thunderheads loomed blackly to the west. Lightning darted forked tongues among their masses. The mutter of the oncoming storm drifted through the night.

"My goodness!" Stacy chattered. "I didn't expect to land in the middle of nowhere."

"And in the middle of the night to boot," her mother moaned. "Where in heaven's name are we, young man? I've seen graveyards that looked more promising."

Their eyes adjusted to the darkness. They found themselves standing near the clay platform that extended in front of Buffalo Bend's depot, which had once been a boxcar. A dimmed lamp burned inside, but the door to the tiny station was locked.

Beyond the station the scattered buildings of a cross-trail settlement formed a ragged pattern beneath the stars. The spidery trace of a wagon road came out of the plain to the south. Another trail glinted pale-white in the darkness, flanking the railroad track east and west. To the north, Vance made out the brush line of a sizable stream. Evidently the Platte River.

"I took it for granted Buffalo Bend would be bigger," Stacy lamented.

Vance removed his hat, ran his fingers through his hair, and said. "Some day I'll learn to keep my big mouth shut. I know why you're here. Don't bother telling me."

"Of course you know," Stacy said acidly. "You said certain persons might be watching the trains at Platte City for anyone who looked like they might have come from Del Rosa."

"But I didn't figure—"

"It does seem to me you might have picked a better place," Stacy said. "This looks positively dismal. Does anyone really live here?"

"As I was saying, it didn't occur to me that I'd have a pair of females on my hands who didn't have the brains to—"

Amanda Fitzroy interrupted him. "It would be better to discuss your mistakes later, young man. That storm is moving this way. It's going to rain pitchforks in a minute or two. We'll be drenched if we stand here talking. We must find a hotel."

Vance gazed around and laughed helplessly.

"Hotel? If you ask me, it hasn't been too many years since the Sioux and the Cheyenne were lifting scalps around here."

"We've got to find *something!*" Stacy exclaimed. "We're bushed. We haven't had a decent night's sleep since we left home. There must be shelter somewhere."

"Would a buffalo wallow do?" Vance snarled.

Lightning flashed nearby. Thunder roared overhead. He peered through the ensuing blackness. The flash of lightning had marked out the shape of a sizable, barn-like structure beyond the depot. It was flanked by a wire-fenced enclosure in which stood freight wagons. He had glimpsed a pole corral where mules were drifting toward the lee of the big structure.

"There's our buffalo wallow!" he exclaimed, gathering luggage in both arms. "Run!"

They raced toward the possible shelter. Lightning glared white over the landscape giving them a clearer inventory of Buffalo Bend. The structure toward which they were heading was a massive wagon barn. Beyond it the settlement consisted of half a dozen houses, one of which was a shed-roofed, small structure that was a store. That seemed to be all. Not a light showed. Buffalo Bend was sound asleep.

They reached the wagon tunnel in the barn as the first spatter of rain struck the plank walls. Lightning illuminated the interior. Two

Concord mudwagons and a full coach were stored to the left, along with other, smaller wheeled equipment. Hoofs stirred in stalls to the right. Hay hung in festoons from a double loft overhead. Long ears of Missouri mules formed a picket line at the opposite end of the wagon tunnel where bars prevented the stock from entering the structure.

Thunder cannonaded overhead. Rain came in a torrent. "Looks like this might be a stagecoach and freight outfit," Vance said during a moment when he could make himself heard.

"The Buffalo Bend Division of Wells Fargo, most likely," Stacy remarked.

"Could be," Vance said. "Do you ladies mind having mules for company?"

"I could think of worse," Amanda Fitzroy said. "The accommodations are not what might be called luxurious, but they are certainly superior to a buffalo wallow. Just what are your plans for reaching Platte City from this place, Mr. Jar— pardon me, I mean, Mr. Harding."

"I had sort of figured I might hop a ride on a freight train," Vance said. "Or maybe take a local passenger train east. I doubt if anybody in Platte City would be much interested in people coming in from this direction on a local train."

"I'm afraid hopping freight trains isn't in my line," Amanda Fitzroy said. "The local train would be more suitable. Is there any way of finding out when, and if, one of the infernal things ever stops at this forsaken place?"

"I have a schedule in my pocket which I consulted long ago," Vance said. "If I recall correctly, a local train goes through Buffalo Bend at 6:45 in the morning. I'll check for sure at daybreak."

"I fear that, tired as we are, Anastasia and I will be awake," she said. "We must certainly be aboard that train if it pauses here. I do not believe the accommodations here are such as to make us eager to stay over."

The full fury of the storm burst. Thunder boomed, lightning played vividly. Rain cascaded on the roof and found openings to drip inside.

The outburst subsided. Vance located a ladder which led to a hayloft. "Speaking of accommodations, Mrs. Fitzroy," he said, "welcome to Hotel Buffalo Bend. I can show you ladies to our very best, second-floor room. With a view."

"You have mistaken me for someone else," Amanda Fitzroy said. "I am Mrs. Jenny Royce from Louisville, Kentucky. Shall I register?"

"That won't be necessary, ma'am. It's an honor to have a lady from the Blue Grass country as a guest."

"What about you?" she asked.

"I'll take a room on the first floor," Vance chuckled. "It might cause scandal otherwise."

Amanda laughed. "We must not have that, above all, must we?"

"It's a subject that should not have even been mentioned," Stacy said severely. "Just keep your thoughts to yourself, Mr. Harding."

She added, "Besides, we're staying down here also, Mother. If you think I'm going to sleep in a haymow, you're mistaken."

"Why, for pity's sake?" her mother demanded. "Surely, you're not afraid of scandal?"

"Something much worse," Stacy said. "Mice."

Her mother uttered a small scream. "Of course! Haymows are always alive with them! I forgot!"

Vance sighed. The storm was passing eastward. Only the pale glimmer of the fading lightning reached inside the barn. "Mice!" he said resignedly. "And you two want to track down murderers!"

He opened the door of the stored big Concord coach. He found a gunnysack and dusted off the seats. "This is our next-best room," he said. "I can't say too much for the size of the beds, but people have been known to sleep on them. At least on this trip your room won't hit any chuckholes to rustle your bustles."

"You see, Mother," Stacy said, "he *is* a rude character."

"Indeed he is," Amanda Fitzroy agreed. "But also very practical."

He helped Amanda into the coach. He halted

Stacy when she was about to follow. "You mentioned that you had learned something else in addition to Roy's murder," he said.

"I did," she said. "It might mean something, it might not. I went over every detail with my father once again. It was not the easiest task I've attempted. He is a stubborn man and was certain he'd already told me everything. Just by accident, he happened to mention that those three boxes of money had been stored overnight in the safe of a bank in Platte City. The name of the bank was the Stockman's Trust Bank."

"But I understood—"

"That Dad and the others had never let the boxes out of their sight. It turns out that wasn't exactly the case. They did see the boxes locked in the big safe, and were present the next morning when the safe was opened. He hadn't believed this was worth mentioning when we talked it over before."

Vance drew a long breath. "So that's when it was done!"

"It looks like it could be the key," she said.

"Who was in charge when the boxes were placed in the safe?" Vance asked.

"The cashier. A man named Harvey Lemmon. But Dad said he trusts Harvey Lemmon. He says he's never made a mistake in judging human nature."

Her mother uttered a sniff. "Much as I love your father, dear," she said, "he couldn't pick a bad apple out of a quart of huckleberries."

"Did he find out why you were questioning him so closely about what happened at Platte City?" Vance asked Stacy.

"I think he began to suspect something, but I managed to avoid telling him the truth."

"This Harvey Lemmon must have been in on switching the boxes," Vance said. "Maybe I can shove him around a little until he talks."

"I doubt if it will be that simple," she said. "If he was in on this thing, he probably isn't the kind who would be easy to shove. Furthermore, there's always the chance it didn't happen that way at all, and that he had nothing to do with it. We're only jumping to a conclusion."

"I've got a dollar that says we're right and that Mr. Harvey Lemmon knows the whole story, and that he'll talk—with the right persuasion."

The last mutter of thunder had died. Rain dripped dismally from the eaves. Stars were reappearing. Stacy ascended into the coach and settled down on the worn cushions opposite her mother.

"Good night!" Vance said. "Sweet dreams."

"Good night!" they replied in unison.

He found clean straw, spread a bed and stretched out. The storm had ended the muggy heat and cleaned the air. Crickets resumed their refrain. Somewhere in the settlement a dog began barking. He drifted off to sleep.

He awakened almost immediately. A horse was passing by at a trot. The animal halted not far away. Wet saddle leather creaked. A hand knocked on a door. Evidently the rider had dismounted at a house that stood just beyond the freight yard.

"Tim!" a muffled voice called.

A man's sleep-thick response came. Vance heard the hinges of a door squeak.

A six-shooter crashed three times. A dying man uttered a blood-drowned sound. Then came the thud of a body falling. The drum of hoofs arose.

Vance ran to the opening in the barn in time to glimpse a rider spurring a horse past by the way he had come. Hoofs spattered mud. A faint, distant flicker of lightning came on the eastern horizon from the retreating storm, vaguely outlining the horseman. He wore a black slicker and had a rain-soggy hat pulled low.

The horseman vanished into the blackness of the night. For a space there was utter silence. Vance crouched, staring, appalled by the realization he had heard the sounds of murder. The picture of that ghostly figure, brief though had been the glimpse, remained in his mind. There had been something about the posture of the man that tantalized him. Somewhere he had seen a person carry himself like that.

187

He found Stacy and her mother at his side, breathing hard with excitement. "What was it?" Stacy chattered. "What happened?"

"I'm not sure," Vance whispered.

A woman began screaming in the settlement. "Help! Help! Tim's been shot! He's been murdered! He's dead! Help!"

12

Buffalo Bend awakened. Voices sounded. Neighbors emerged from houses and ran to where the woman kept screaming. The screams changed to grievous sobbing.

"He's dead!" a man spoke hoarsely, incredulously. "Tim's dead!"

A babble arose. Questions that had no answers. Confusion, disbelief, horror. And more grief. The tracks of the slayer's horses were hunted, but the pools of rain had covered them. A telegraph key began rattling in the box car depot. The station agent, in his pants and nightshirt, was wiring the news to the sheriff in the county seat.

"Oh, the poor man!" Amanda Fitzroy moaned. "From what I heard, he seemed to have been the stable boss of this very place we are in."

"What will we do now?" Stacy asked.

"The haymow," Vance said. "Mice or no mice."

"Now, I don't see why—" she began.

"If we're caught here, we'll have to do a lot of explaining. We would likely be held as witnesses, even though what we know wouldn't be of any real help. The fat would be in the fire then, as far as any snooping in Platte City is concerned. We'd have to tell who we really are."

"The haymow it is," Stacy decided. She added

plaintively, "And you're staying with us. Do you hear?"

"Gallantly I will see to it that no mice get within squeaking distance of either of you," Vance promised.

"That poor man!" her mother repeated. "How awful! It was cold-blooded murder. I wonder why he was killed?"

"No telling," Vance said. He raked his mind, still nagged by the memory of the glimpse he had of the slayer. But its substance continued to elude him.

He helped Amanda Fitzroy ascend to the mow. Stacy quickly mounted the ladder. He handed up their luggage, then joined them. He covered the luggage with hay and arranged hollows into which the three of them could cover themselves in case of necessity.

Otherwise, they prowled the half-empty interior of the mow, listening and peering from knotholes and weather slits. Sleep was impossible. Buffalo Bend remained aboil.

No one approached the stage barn. "But there'll be hostlers showing up after daybreak to take care of the stock," Vance said. "We'll have to change camp before that happens. At first chance we better try to scuttle to the brush along the river and wait for the local to pull in."

Buffalo Bend calmed after a few hours. Vance left the barn to scout the feasibility of moving to a new hiding place. "All right," he said when he returned. "I've found a brushy patch between the river and the railroad track that looks like it might be made to order. No smoking, drinking or cussing. If anybody tries to question us, I'll pretend I don't know you. You'll have to think up your own fables."

They reached the thicket unseen and Vance led the way into a small clearing that evidently must have been tramped down by range cattle in the past.

"You neglected to mention mosquitoes," Stacy said, slapping vigorously. "I swear, I'd almost rather take my chances with mice."

Daybreak finally came. The sun arose. Luck was with them in one respect. The local train pulled in on schedule. It consisted of a combination baggage and mail car, two ancient wooden coaches that looked like they dated back to the days of Indian fighting, and two stock cars loaded with sheep.

The train halted at the box car depot which was abreast of their hideout. Evidently the citizens of Buffalo Bend were out in force on the settlement-side of the train, shouting the story of the night's excitement, for the attention of the trainmen and the passengers was concentrated in that direction.

Vance and his companions left their hiding place and approached the train unseen. He

191

boosted Amanda Fitzroy up the steps of one of the coaches. He attempted to perform the same service for Stacy. She slapped his hands away. "You'd take any advantage, wouldn't you?" she hissed.

He handed up the luggage and they entered the coach and slid quietly into seats. The train finally jolted into motion. Stacy uttered a small exhausted sigh of triumph, rolling her eyes thankfully.

The conductor eventually discovered their presence and was properly incredulous. He was a horny-handed, red-jowled Irishman, with the arrogance of minor authority. "Sure, an' where did the likes o' ye three git aboard?" he demanded.

Vance had consulted his train schedule and was prepared for that. "Conway," he said, naming a station west of Buffalo Bend. "We'll buy fare to Platte City."

The conductor scowled and blew through his sandy mustache, but did not dare question the statement, for it implied that he had been amiss in his vigilance. He named the amount. His scowl deepened to total disapproval when Stacy opened her purse and produced the money to cover the cost.

" 'Tis not often I have come across a man who lets a lady pay his expenses," he snorted as he counted out the change.

"I don't know which one I ought to punch in the nose," Vance growled after the man had gone away. "Him or you. I've still got some money. After this, let me at least act like a gentleman."

"I took it for granted that you'd blown in all I gave you on ruffled shirts and rainbow vests," she said.

Vance sat in glum silence. The train made many stops, and lay over for more than thirty minutes for a string of empty cattle cars that were westbound. It was past midmorning when the conductor came into their car, gave them a glare, and bawled, "Platte City, next stop! Platte City!"

The train had picked up many fares along the way, and more than a score of passengers alighted along with them, giving them a measure of security in numbers. Vance took advantage of the opportunity to seize their luggage and head for a dilapidated carryall that waited at the depot. It transported them and half a dozen other arrivals up the street toward a hotel.

Platte City was larger and busier than Vance had suspected from his glimpse the previous evening. Many stores were active. Freight wagons, ranch rigs, buckboards and mounted men crowded the street. A side street was given over to gambling houses and music halls, although that area was almost deserted at this hour.

Their vehicle stopped at a large hostelry in the heart of town whose sign named it VICTORIA HOUSE. Three of the occupants alighted, but Vance spoke to the driver. "This looks like you have to pay extra for the gingerbread and the fancy. What's the next best?"

"Just a minute!" Stacy exclaimed. "This is—"

"Quit acting like a Fitzroy!" Vance murmured. "You're a girl looking for a job—and a husband—remember. You don't want to draw suspicion by acting too much like you were born with a gold spoon in your mouth, do you?"

The driver was gazing scornfully at Vance. "The Plains House ought to be cheap enough for yore purse," he said.

Vance leaned forward, a tight little smile on his lips, a fist knotting. Stacy grasped his arm and pulled him back. "Remember," she murmured chidingly. "No violence. As you just said, we don't want to call attention to ourselves, now do we?"

The Plains House was an ugly, flat-roofed, oblong structure with a rickety balcony on the second floor that overhung Platte City's principal street. However, inside, it proved to be clean enough, but without flourish.

Stacy and her mother, after some dickering, rented a bedroom and sitting room on the upper floor at the front. Vance selected a room, which was also on the second floor, but at the rear.

194

They gave the clerk the impression they were only casual acquaintances who had happened to arrive on the same train.

Vance shaved and bathed. Afterward, making sure the hall was vacant, he walked to the Fitzroy rooms and tapped. Stacy admitted him. She had abandoned the corkscrew curls and yellow shoes and changed to a simple lawn dress and slippers.

"That's a considerable improvement," Vance said, inspecting her from head to foot.

"I regret I can't say the same for you," she said. "Is that hideous rainbow vest really necessary?"

"You've darkened my day," he said. "Attire like this is worn by all the very best shell-game sharpers and tinhorn gamblers. Fact is, it's always been one of my secret ambitions to own a vest of this distinctive aspect. In some circles it is considered attractive."

"Then you can consider that you've lived life to the full," she commented. "There is obviously nothing more for you to look forward to."

Her mother appeared from the bedroom. Like Stacy, she had changed to simple attire. She seemed years younger, more vibrant, more vital. She watched Vance's expression. "Thank you, young man," she said. "I see that you approve of me. All this excitement is good for me."

"If you're as starved as I am," he said, "it's time you had breakfast. There's an eating place almost across the street that looks satisfactory.

We can't be seen there together, of course. Its name is the Palace Cafe."

"There seems to be a lot of excitement in the other direction down the street," Stacy said, gazing from a window. "Look!"

Vance joined her. About a block west, a jostling line of men and women looped along the sidewalk from the door of a stone-faced structure whose windows bore gilt lettering that Vance could not read at that distance. The place, however, was obviously a bank.

"Looks like a run on a bank," he said. "But it seems to be paying off. Its doors are still open."

As they watched it became obvious the panic was subsiding. Many began quitting the line. A man wearing the sleeveguards of a teller stood in the bank's door, smiling and exuding confidence.

"Looks like a false alarm," Vance said. "Meanwhile I only grow hungrier. I'll see you later."

Stacy continued to peer. "The name of the bank," she said, "is the Stockman's Trust Bank. That is where the beef money was left in the safe overnight."

Vance paused. "Well, well," he said thoughtfully. "Now do you suppose we've struck a glimmer of paydirt?"

He left the room and made his way to the Palace Cafe. The last of the dwindling line of depositors was entering the door of the bank down the street.

A plump, blonde waitress was very busy, for the majority of the tables in the restaurant were occupied. A sign had been pasted on the street window: WAITRESS WANTED!

The lone waitress finally got to his table. "What was all the excitement at the bank down the street?" he asked.

Big news took precedence even over the demands of her duties and she paused to talk. "People got scared when they heard about Harvey Lemmon, an' thought the bank might have been in trouble, so they came runnin' to get their money out. But the bank is sound. They been payin' off every cent all mornin'."

"What happened to Harvey Lemmon?" Vance asked.

"Haven't you heard? They found his body in the river early this mornin'. At first they thought he'd committed suicide. Now they say he's been murdered."

"Harvey Lemmon," Vance said mechanically, "was cashier at the Stockman's Trust Bank, wasn't he?"

"He sure was," the waitress said. "An' well liked in this town. You must be a stranger around here, mister. Now, I got to take your order. We're shorthanded."

"Ham and," Vance said. "Eggs over and well. Black coffee."

She hurried away. Vance saw that Stacy and

her mother had entered the restaurant. Stacy paused to speak to the man who presided at the cash till. It was quite a conversation. The man, who evidently was also the owner of the place, finally nodded. He turned and removed the WAITRESS WANTED sign from the window.

Stacy's mother moved to a table and took a chair. She gave Vance a fleeting side-glance, her eyes lifting resignedly heavenward, as though she was washing her hands of responsibility.

The owner led Stacy through the swing doors into the kitchen at the rear. Presently she reappeared, wearing a starched apron similar to the one on the buxom waitress who began giving her instructions in the art of waiting table.

Stacy was assigned an area that included Vance's table. One of her first duties was to bring his plate of ham and eggs.

"Remember Harvey Lemmon?" he murmured.

"Of course," she breathed.

"He'll never be able to tell us anything," Vance said. "He's been murdered. That was the cause of all the rush on the bank."

She stared at him, trying to determine the significance of the news. Vance shrugged. "I don't know any more than that." He raised his voice. "Nope, no sugar an' cream, dearie, even though I can see you've got plenty of the same."

"Don't be too much of a ham," she murmured.

"You're being carried away by your role as a tinhorn."

"Maybe we can go for a buggy ride one of these evenings, dearie!" Vance said.

"Don't hold your breath until we do," she said.

Vance finished his breakfast and left the restaurant. There were still half a dozen or more persons on the sidewalk in front of the Stockman's Trust Bank, but they were only talking. The run on the teller's cage had ended. Vance walked in that direction.

Standing at street level, he could see into the lobby. Gold coin and greenbacks were stacked in plain sight in the open door of a massive safe that was set into the wall of the bank—the same safe, no doubt, in which the beef money had been left for safekeeping overnight. This display of wealth was the customary method of a bank seeking to reassure its depositors that it could meet its obligations. In this case the plan had been successful, for the run was over.

His first thought was that the bank had been paying off with the stolen beef money. He doubted this, but could not find proof one way or another. He finally strolled to a pool hall and took a seat. He lingered for an hour or more in the place, along with four or five other idlers whose way of life apparently consisted of avoiding manual labor at all costs.

The murder of Harvey Lemmon was, of course, the major topic, but when it was all sifted down they knew nothing more than what he had already heard.

However, a cautious change of subject brought out the fact that the citizens of Platte City had heard of the theft of the beef money down in Texas, and of the fact the loot was fresh mintage and easy to identify. The story had been published in the local newspaper. That exploded the possibility the bank might have used the stolen money to bolster its position.

The gambling line, which was confined to a cross street, labeled Sundown Street, did not begin to stir until late afternoon. He made his way there as twilight came and bought chips in a small-limit draw poker game in a gambling trap named the Hornspoon. The game was slow, with luck about even. The house dealer, a bored old-timer who had no use for strangers who came in wearing cheap tinhorn garb, kept yawning and watching the clock, waiting for the time to close the game and go home to the supper his wife was cooking, a matter that he kept mentioning.

Vance lost a little, won a little. He dropped out of every hand in which he did not have an early advantage, hoarding his meager stake in the true piker tradition. He was establishing himself in their minds as a drifter who lived on the thin edge and who was hardly worth attention. He listened to all the talk around.

The main subject, of course, was still the murder of Harvey Lemmon and the run on the bank. Vance learned that the cashier's body had been found by a hunter, lodged in driftwood above town on the Platte River.

Lemmon had been seen driving out of town the previous evening. His horse and top buggy had been found near the river a distance above where the body had been discovered. Lemmon had been shot in the back.

"Buck Joseph has got his hands full, fer sure," someone remarked. "There was another killin' upriver at Buffalo Bend durin' the night. Tim Murphy, the barn boss fer the stage company, was called to the door o' his home after he'd gone to bed, an' was blasted down with a six-gun. Buck was just about to ketch the westbound local when Harvey Lemmon's murder turned up. So Buck sent his deputy, Frank Archer, down to the Bend to look into the killin' there."

"I seen Tim Murphy here in Platte City only a couple days ago," another poker player said. "Seen him havin' a drink right here in this bar. Now I wonder who'd have grudge enough ag'in old Tim to rub him out?"

Vance learned that Buck Joseph was sheriff of the county. He presently cashed in his chips and drifted to another gambling house. Then another.

It was nearing midnight when he finally gave it up for the night and left Sundown Street, heading for the Plains House.

The Palace Cafe was closed. A night lamp burned in the lobby of the hotel. He felt his weariness as he mounted to the second floor. However, he saw lamplight showing beneath the door of the quarters Stacy and her mother occupied.

He tapped on the door. It was quickly opened by Stacy, who admitted him to the sitting room and closed and bolted the door. It was evident she had been awaiting him. The door to the bedroom stood open. A lamp burned there.

"Mother's still awake," Stacy said. "Did you learn anything about the death of Harvey Lemmon?"

"Nothing more than that he drove out of town yesterday afternoon, and his body was found in the river about daybreak this morning. Someone had shot him in the back. That's about it, except that I learned they don't particularly care for penny ante pikers in their games. And you?"

"Nothing, except that a nickel tip is supposed to give certain males the right to take liberties," she sighed.

"Maybe you ought to shoot one or two," Vance said. "Just to establish a principle."

"I may try that later. I have nice, strong finger-nails and had to use them on one occasion."

"What would Major Webster Fitzroy think if he knew his daughter was slinging hash in a cowtown beanery?"

"I forbid Anastasia to continue working in that awful place." Her mother spoke from the adjoining room. "My husband would die of shame."

"I earned a whole dollar and forty cents today," Stacy said. "Minus twenty cents for broken dishes, of course."

"They dock you for that?"

"Indeed they do. Sim Dutton is not a man to let a penny slip through his fingers. He's the owner."

"Even so you came out better than I did," Vance admitted. "I'm two dollars out at poker. It's been a losing day all around. I'll say good-night now."

He turned to leave, then paused as though struck by an afterthought. "By the way, here's the derringer you loaned me. I won't need it, but your mother might want to keep it handy in case some drunk tries to get gay."

Stacy reluctantly accepted the weapon, but her mother spoke. "Stacy might need it against those mashers in the Palace Cafe, but I'm already adequately armed, and not with a peashooter like that. I have a .45 that will permanently discourage any scoundrel, I assure you."

She added, "And let's call a spade a spade.

203

We both know what you really mean, young man. There could be only one answer to Harvey Lemmon's murder. He was eliminated, either because they were afraid he might talk, or that they didn't want to have to split the money up with him. Perhaps for both reasons. Whoever put Harvey Lemmon and Roy Carvell out of the way will do the same to any person they suspect may be a danger to them. We are dealing with a ruthless person. Or persons. I'm sure you both know that as well as I do. So be very careful, Mr. Harding. And we will be also. Goodnight now. Pleasant dreams."

"The same to both of you," Vance said. "And keep some furniture wedged against the door."

He returned to Sundown Street the next evening and sat in occasionally at the poker or monte tables or sipped beer at the bars. He listened to the talk and struck up conversations with anyone who seemed even remotely likely to offer a word that might lead to something.

It was a futile night. About all he learned was that the directors of the Stockman's Trust Bank had offered a reward of two thousand dollars for information that would lead to the arrest of the murderer of Harvey Lemmon. Sundown Street was alive with rumors and theories, but that was all it amounted to. Talk. Wild flights of the imagination. At last he gave it up again, and returned to the hotel. Stacy and her mother, once more, were awaiting his report.

"Not a damned, blasted thing," he told them.

"The same here," she said glumly. "I've eavesdropped on so many private conversations I'm growing ears like a jackrabbit. And the things I've overheard. I wouldn't repeat them in mixed company. But not a word that would help us."

Harvey Lemmon's funeral was held the next day. The procession was half a mile long and the services at the grave lasted until late in the afternoon.

"Almost everybody in town turned out," Stacy commented when they held their conference late that night. "Surely, if he is a crook, he couldn't have been that popular."

"Maybe they were there for the same reason I was," Vance said.

"You were among the mourners? Why, for pity's sake?"

"As a boy I heard of an old saying that the spirit of the dead would arise and mark the guilt of any false mourner who came to a grave. If the mark was placed on any of them, it escaped my attention. All I saw was a blur of beards and mustaches. And it was mighty hot standing in the sun two hours."

"Maybe we better try tea leaves, or read the cards," Amanda Fitzroy said caustically. "If we have fallen to hoping the departed spirits will

205

help us, then I say we are indeed on a wild goose chase."

Another barren day passed. And another. Harvey Lemmon's murder was already becoming a thing of the past, an unsolved mystery and fading in public interest. The killing of the stagecoach company's barn boss at Buffalo Bend was even more quickly forgotten.

Interest shifted to more recent events. Two cowboys fought a gun battle over a percentage girl in a dancehall on Sundown Street, one going to his grave, the other to the hospital. That became the new topic of the day.

Vance met Stacy and her mother once again, after a futile week. "All I'm likely to get out of this are fallen arches," Stacy sighed. "At least I've upped my daily income to almost three dollars, mainly in tips."

"I've heard about the new beauty who's slinging hash at the Palace," Vance said. "She's the talk of the town. Have you had any proposals of marriage lately?"

"Not of marriage," she said coldly.

Vance patronized the Palace Cafe only occasionally, not wanting anyone to suspect there might be a close link between him and the comely new waitress. However, the next day he decided to take his noon meal there.

The tables were filled, and he found a vacancy at the counter at the rear. Stacy was busy. Vance noted that she had also become proficient in her duties. She hadn't complained of being docked for broken dishes in several days.

Four cowhands with payday money in their pockets occupied a table. They had started their drinking early, and it was evident they had come to the Palace especially to learn if stories about the beautiful new waitress were true. She tried to avoid hands as she brought food.

An arm tried to encircle her waist. She slapped the annoyer with a pistol-shot report. The blow drove the cowboy back in his chair. His companions guffawed, and that enraged him. He reared up, determined to corner Stacy and embrace her.

Other diners sat staring, refraining from interfering, knowing from past experience that here were the elements of a table-smashing, window-busting brawl. Furthermore, the four cowboys were armed.

Vance sat calmly eating his food, ignoring the scene. Stacy sent him an angry look of appeal. He continued to remain aloof. She glared daggers. He remained oblivious of her plight.

She acted on her own behalf. She seized a plate filled with beef stew from the table and hurled it in the face of her tormenter. She next struck him over the head with the plate, smashing it. Her stunned victim staggered back, tripped over his own feet and crashed to the floor.

She seized another plate, ready to continue the battle, but at that moment Buck Joseph, the sheriff, came charging into the place and interceded. He evicted the stew-spattered cowhand and warned his companions to sober up or spend the next month in jail. The dejected quartet vanished in the direction of Sundown Street, leaving Stacy victorious on the field of combat. She gave Vance a look of utter scorn.

She was very short and acrimonious toward him that night when they held their customary confab in the sitting room at the hotel. "That was the most craven thing I ever saw in a human being," she stated. "Provided you consider yourself in that category. Where is your chivalry?"

"I must have misplaced it," Vance said. "I'll look around for it."

"Why didn't you help me against those saddle bums?"

"It looked to me like they were the ones who needed help. Anyway, one of us in the limelight is enough. Too much, I'm afraid."

"Don't change the subject," she fumed. "I still say you're about as ornery a—"

"I'm not changing the subject. What I'm trying to tell you and your mother is that you both better clear out of Platte City and head for home."

She was taken aback. "Now, why? Just tell me that?"

"You're becoming too famous," Vance said. "The toast of Platte City. Cowboys are riding miles out of their way to view the pretty waitress at the Palace. When word gets around how you crowned that puncher with a plate of stew, Sim Dutton will be charging admission to let the customers in."

"That's ridiculous. Anyway, I won't admit we're beaten yet."

"I didn't say we were beaten, I only say that, sooner or later, somebody is likely to savvy that the beautiful hash slinger who busts plates over the heads of mashers might not be exactly what she pretends. They might start making inquiries. Then something unlucky might happen to her."

Stacy swallowed hard but refused to be daunted. "On the other hand," she argued, "if I'm as notorious as all that, maybe I'll hear something that may unravel this thing."

Vance uttered a groan of anguish. "Don't you ever give in? You may be in danger! It was coincidence that we happened to practically witness that murder at Buffalo Bend, but we all know it was not exactly coincidence that the man was murdered shortly after Harvey Lemmon was put out of the way. Somebody had to furnish those three express boxes to whoever exchanged them while they were in the bank safe. Wells Fargo just doesn't let their equipment lie around loose for anyone to use. Tim Murphy, being a barn boss, and living far enough from Platte City to avoid suspicion, was likely the one who furnished those items to the someone, or the someones we're hunting. His reward was to be killed for the same reason Harvey Lemmon and Roy Carvell were murdered. To silence him for keeps, and to avoid having to give him any share of the money."

He paused, then added quietly, "In other words, as I mentioned before, we all know our opposition will stop at nothing—murder least of all. They've already killed three times."

"Stop glaring at me that way!" Stacy said testily. "I'm scared, if that satisfies you. But I'm staying, and that's that. If anybody leaves Platte City, it should be you."

"Me? Do you know what you're saying?"

"If you ask me," she said, "I doubt if anybody really believes that tinhorn role you're trying to play."

"At least I'm not counting on anybody taking a shine to me and asking me to help spend a hundred thousand dollars on a good time," Vance raged. He arose, kicked the chair in which he had been sitting across the room, and left, heading for his own quarters.

13

A s darkness came the following day, Vance stood at the bar of the Hornspoon in Sundown Street, sipping a glass of mineral water, attentive to the conversation around him, without appearing to be listening—an art that was becoming a habit with him.

With another part of his mind he was trying to decide whether to have supper at the Palace Cafe, or to patronize some other establishment. He decided on the Palace, even though he had become an increasingly frequent patron there. It had become a legitimate excuse for watching over Stacy.

He had a gambler's hunch that events were closing in on them, and not in their favor. He had desperately hoped that Stacy would heed his wishes and get out of danger along with her mother. How desperately he did not want to admit, even to himself. Stacy Fitzroy was beginning to fill all his world, cloud all his thoughts.

He had a view through the front window into Sundown Street. The window was fitted with a blind that extended from the bottom. It was fulfilling its purpose, being raised only part way so that patrons inside could see into the street while passersby would have only a dim view of faces and shoulders within.

A rider came off Trail Street into Sundown Street, halted his horse at the rail of a gambling house across the way, and dismounted.

Vance straightened, his breath catching. Something in the posture of the arrival struck fire in his mind. The horseman wore the commonplace garb of a rancher—cotton shirt, worn black vest, dark trousers bagged over cowboots, sand-colored, wide-brimmed hat. It was the set of his shoulders, their stiff forward thrust that held Vance rigidly motionless, staring.

The arrival tethered his horse and turned so that the lamplight from the gambling house window touched his face.

Vance spoke to a man who stood next to him at the bar, drinking a mug of beer. "Say, that looks like an old tillicum of mine that I used to play poker with up on Wind River. Name of Tom Jeffers."

He was indicating the arrival, who was now moving toward the door of the opposite establishment. Vance's neighbor peered. "I reckon yo're mistook, mister," he said. "Thet's Sid Kelso. He's Big Mike Deavers's partner in a spread up the river a piece."

Kelso! Vance stood there thinking of Len Kelso, who, along with a mysterious partner who had given the name of Sam Jones, had talked

Roy Carvell into helping steal the counterfeit treasure boxes at the Fitzroy ranch.

He was remembering the man he had played poker with at the Blue Star that night in Del Rosa a few hours before the robbery—the man who had said his name was Ed Walsh. Sam Jones, Ed Walsh and Sid Kelso were one and the same. He knew now why Walsh's features had been tantalizingly familiar that night. Sid Kelso and Len Kelso were probably brothers.

The wild goose chase was no longer a maze. The pieces in the jigsaw puzzle had suddenly moved into place.

"It must have been the way the light hit him," Vance said, fighting to keep his voice casual. "On second glance, I can see he really don't look much like old Tom Jeffers after all."

He added, "What did you say his name was? Kelly?"

"Kelso," his neighbor corrected him. "Sid Kelso." The man was in a mood to be talkative. "Not that I ain't sayin' Sid might have used another name in the past," he murmured confidentially. "He ain't got a reputation for bein' what you might call a pillar o' rectitude. Nor his pardner, Big Mike Deavers, neither."

"Sounds interesting," Vance commented. "What sort of a spread do they operate?"

"They're supposed to run enough cattle to keep 'em in likker an' women, but I've heard say that steers in the Blockhouse iron are mighty scarce. Anyway, Kelso an' Big Mike seem to eat regular an' there's been some high old times at Blockhouse, so I hear."

"Blockhouse?"

"It was an old Army post durin' the Injun days. Kelso an' Big Mike tuk it over cheap years ago. It's about eight, nine miles out below Needle Buttes, west o' town."

Vance and the talkative one drifted apart. Vance watched the door of the gambling house that Sid Kelso had entered. He never let it out of his sight.

A quarter of an hour passed. Half an hour. He could curb his impatience no longer. He left the Hornspoon, crossed the street and paused outside the gambling house. He was in shadow, but could survey the interior over the tops of the batwing doors.

Sid Kelso was just rising from a chair at a monte table. He cashed in his chips and headed toward the door to leave the place, moving with that forward push of his shoulders that marked him.

Vance hastily retreated, heading down the sidewalk, keeping to the shadows as much as possible. He glanced over his shoulder as the man emerged from the swing doors. Sid Kelso did not look in his direction, but mounted his horse. With a rancher's scorn of foot travel, the man rode into Trail Street, where Vance saw him tether his mount in front of the Palace Cafe and enter the eating place.

Thus was Vance's hunch being fulfilled. Some fatalistic foresight in him had told him it would turn out this way. Striding fast, he reached a dark doorway across the street from the restaurant where he had a view of the interior.

Kelso had taken a seat at a table. And, of course, the table was one that Stacy was serving. That was the way fate was now arranging affairs, Vance reflected.

The only question now was whether Kelso had seen Stacy when he had been in Del Rosa under the name of Ed Walsh. Seen her long enough to remember her and know she was not Stella Royce, but the daughter of Major Webster Fitzroy.

Kelso was studying the blackboard on the wall where the menu was chalked. Stacy came to the table bearing a tumbler of water and utensils. She primly straightened her starched apron as she awaited Kelso's order. She was completely unaware that before her sat the man who might murder her.

Kelso made his decision and turned his attention to Stacy. His first reaction was appreciation of her scenic virtues. Then Vance saw a subtle change. Kelso was racking his mind, trying to place her in his memory.

Then he knew! And he surely must have reasoned, in the next moment, her purpose for being here in Platte City working as a waitress. And he most certainly could see that she did not know he was the person she was seeking.

Kelso lowered his head to hide any sign of his discovery. He must have given some order, for Stacy moved away, heading for the kitchen. She quickly returned, bearing a bowl of soup—the order a man would first think of in an emergency.

Kelso was careful to keep his face away from her, but Vance saw that his eyes were roving the room, judging the patrons. The man's glance moved to the window, scanning the dark street. Vance crouched deeper in his hiding place and was sure he had not been seen by Kelso.

He was following the run of Kelso's thoughts. The man's first surmise was that Stacy had not come to Platte City alone. He was trying to learn if he was being watched by anyone who might have accompanied her from Del Rosa.

Vance waited his chance and moved entirely out of possible range of Kelso's eyes. He kept the door of the Palace under observation at a greater distance. After a few minutes, Kelso emerged and swung into the saddle. Without a backward glance, the man rode down Trail Street westward, apparently heading out of town.

Vance waited until the man had vanished down the street. He started to step from concealment, his first instinct being to warn Stacy. Then a sense of caution prevailed and he crouched down again, waiting until a ranch wagon came down the street, lifting a cloud of dust. With this as a screen, he moved to a better vantage point in a lane between buildings, which gave him a full view of the interior of the Palace Cafe, as well as offering an avenue of retreat for himself.

His caution paid off. He presently spotted Sid Kelso's high-shouldered figure approaching on foot from the east. The man had circled the town, left his mount and had returned to Trail Street from the opposite direction.

Vance retreated deeper into the darkness between the buildings. He watched Kelso pass by. The man was obviously peering into such places, but he did not change pace. Vance was again sure his presence had not been discovered.

He moved to the street again. Kelso was once more entering the Palace Cafe. Vance drew his six-shooter and cocked it, ready to shoot through the window. Kelso took the same chair at the table he had previously occupied. Stacy again came to the table, setting utensils in front of him.

Kelso looked up at her, smiling from his hard, sharp face, and made some remark. Stacy smiled politely in return and waited for his order.

It was a striking insight into the man's character. He had shown that he was coldly intelligent and not easily stampeded. He had circled back to the Palace with two purposes in mind. One was to learn if anyone had approached Stacy to warn her. The other was to make doubly sure that Stacy, herself, had not recognized him as the man who had been in Del Rosa a few hours before the holdup at Oak Hill.

Vance waited, the gun palmed. Kelso, this time, ordered a full meal. He ate with the deliberation of a man whose nerves were well in hand. But Vance was certain the man was watching Stacy's every move, trying to make sure that she had not detected anything out of the ordinary.

Apparently convinced at last, Kelso finished a cup of coffee, left a nickel on the table as a tip, paid his bill at the cashier's stand and left the restaurant. He retraced his way eastward along Trail Street, moving with the unhurried swing of a man at peace with the world. He turned down a side street.

Vance retreated down the lane between structures to this dark back street and saw Kelso mount his horse which he had left there. Once more Kelso rode westward, heading out of town. This time he began to push the horse, once he reached the outskirts. Apparently, he was really on his way out of Platte City.

However, it again might be a trick. Vance returned to his vantage point and kept watch on the Palace Cafe—and on Stacy as she moved about in the place. It was a long vigil. There was no sign that Sid Kelso had returned, but there was always the chance he might be waiting in hiding somewhere for Stacy to appear from the restaurant when it closed for the night. Waiting to kill her.

Vance entered the Palace fifteen minutes before closing time and ordered a doughnut and a cup of coffee. Stacy waited on him.

"Leave by the back door," he murmured. He added quickly, "Don't ask questions—now!"

He was waiting in the dusty alley at the rear of the Palace when she emerged. He motioned her to walk ahead and followed her at a dozen paces, his pistol in his hand. She reached the Plains House unharmed, and Vance decided that Sid Kelso had not returned.

He followed Stacy upstairs to her quarters. Her mother was sitting in a chair, gold-rimmed spectacles canted on her nose, reading a novel.

Vance closed and bolted the door. He eyed the title of the book. "*The Rejected Lover*," he said. "I see you're improving your mind. Where did you get that piece of literature?"

"From the news butcher on the train, if it's any of your business, young man," she said. "However, I'm disappointed in it. There's no information in it that I did not already have."

She watched Vance lower the hammer of his six-shooter and holster the gun. The blind on the front window was only partly drawn. He crossed the room and closed the blind, then drew the curtains, being careful not to expose himself at the window.

"Now!" Stacy breathed. "May I ask a question?"

Vance grinned thinly. "Later. First, you and your mother start packing."

"Packing? Now you're not going to start that again?"

"You two are boarding the first train out of here tomorrow. Meanwhile keep away from any open windows. Don't even let your shadows fall on a curtain."

Amanda Fitzroy spoke. "You've finally stumbled onto something, haven't you?"

"I've found the needle," he said. "Also the haystack. The needle's name is Kelso. Ever hear that name before?"

"Kelso?" Stacy exclaimed. "*Len* Kelso?"

"This one is Sid Kelso. There's a resemblance. They must be brothers. Sid seems to be considerably older than Len. He's a partner in some sort of a shady ranch west of town. They call the place the Blockhouse."

He let that sink in for a moment, watching their expressions. "I see that light is beginning to dawn on both of you, as it has on me," he continued. "This explains a lot of things that were very unclear up to now. I had heard stories that Len was from up in this part of the country, but had to clear out after some kind of a scrape."

"It's all plain enough," Stacy said. "Sid Kelso arranged with that crooked bank cashier, Harvey Lemmon, to exchange the express boxes that night in the bank safe."

Vance nodded. "Then Sid Kelso must have headed for Del Rosa, knowing his brother was living there, and arranged the fake robbery."

"Why did he do that?" Amanda asked.

"To set up a blind trail, no doubt," Vance said. "The law is hunting for the money down in Texas, a thousand miles from Platte City. Nobody but the Kelsos were supposed to know that those express boxes they took from Oak Hill that night were filled only with scrap iron, and that the money was still up here."

He added slowly, "Nobody alive, at least, now that Harvey Lemmon and Tim Murphy and Roy Carvell are in their graves."

"In other words, as I've pointed out before," Amanda Fitzroy said, "they can't be hung any higher for a few more murders. I'm referring to the three of us."

"Why would we be in any danger?" Stacy protested. "I've never laid eyes on this Sid Kelso, and therefore—"

"But you have," Vance said. "Not two hours ago. Remember that hatchet-jawed man with the thin shoulders hiked high that came into the Palace for a bowl of soup, then returned a little later and ordered a full meal? That was Sid Kelso."

She was shaken. "But he could not have known who I was," she said.

"Wrong again. He was in Del Rosa the night of the robbery. I played poker with him. He used the name of Ed Walsh. He was there to set up an alibi. He interfered in my ruckus with Dolph Schneer, even though it was none of his affair. I figure now he wanted witnesses to know he was there. But he quit the poker game early. It was nearly three hours later before the fire was started at Oak Hill. That was time enough for him to have joined up with Len Kelso and my brother-in-law."

"But how would he know me?" she demanded.

"You weren't exactly a wallflower that night when they were celebrating the beef money they thought they were going to get the next day. When he saw you tonight in the restaurant he was so taken aback, he left in a hurry. After he thought it over he came back to make sure he hadn't been imagining things. Then he *was* sure. He knows you're Web Fitzroy's daughter and that you didn't come here for your health. He probably aims to see that your health declines in a hurry by way of a .45 slug, the way Lemmon and Tim Murphy were rubbed out."

She was convinced. Color had receded from her face. "What can we do?" she breathed. "Should we go to the sheriff?"

"What would we tell him? A story about three

express boxes full of junk? About how your father was played for a sucker and fell for it?"

Amanda Fitzroy glared down her nose at him. "I should resent that, young man!" she sniffed. "However, you have a point. The sheriff probably wouldn't believe us. There is no use exposing my husband to further humiliation at the hands of people who don't understand. If we went to the sheriff, it would all have to be told."

"In addition," Vance said, "we've got no actual proof. Only our word. If we went to the law, Sid Kelso would likely get wind of it. He'd bury that hundred thousand dollars so deep we'd never have a chance of seeing it again. Finding that money is our only way of convincing anybody."

"You believe it's still around here?" Stacy asked.

"I'm betting on it. That story you planted about the money being easy to identify seems to be pretty well known. I've heard it mentioned once or twice. But nobody dreams it was important to anybody but the law down in Texas."

"It seems we've come back to the same old needle and haystack," she said glumly. "The haystack may have grown smaller, but it's still a haystack."

"They say a needle will find its way eventually to the center of the haystack," he said. "That word, needle, might be a gambler's hunch. I'll start looking for it at Needle Buttes. That's where I was told Kelso and a man named Big Mike Deavers operate their ranch."

"What do you mean, looking?"

"I thought I'd meander out that way and take a peek at this Blockhouse outfit."

"And I suppose you expect to ride right in and ask them if they stole a hundred thousand dollars from my father?"

"That would be mighty rude, now wouldn't it? They might take umbrage to it."

"Umbrage, bumbrage. You'll get yourself into a grave, Vance Jardine."

"The name is Harding, Miss Royce. And don't look at me like I've just kicked a dog. All I'm going to do is to scout the place from a distance, just to get the lay of the land and to see what it looks like."

"When do we start?" she demanded.

He sighed. Her mother also sighed. "I could have said that for you," he growled. "I knew it was coming."

"And so?"

"Tomorrow."

"In broad daylight?"

"There's no other way. If anybody gets nosy, I'll pretend I'm a cowpuncher riding the chuck-line in search of a job."

Stacy looked him over. "In that tinhorn outfit?"

"I've got other clothes."

Her mother spoke. "You are aware, of course,

that if this man Ed Walsh, or Sid Kelso, or whatever his real name, sights you, the jig is up. Remember, he saw you in Del Rosa. He'll know why you came here, and will act accordingly. With a pistol, knife, ax, or whatever is handy to exterminate you."

"I intend to keep out of his way. And that's what you and your daughter will do. Again I tell you to start packing."

"I don't understand why that's necessary," Stacy objected.

"Kelso is certain to find out that you and your mother are staying here at the Plains House," he explained. "This room might be visited."

"Where could we go?"

"To the Victoria House for the rest of the night, at least. I can't think of any other place. And east by the first train out of here in the morning."

Her mother uttered a sniff of scorn. "I don't intend to be stampeded like a blatting sheep by a ruffian or by a bunch of ruffians. I'm staying right here, young man, and you can consider that subject closed. In any event Anastasia and myself are in no danger." She added grimly, "As long as you are alive, that is."

"You have a spooky way of putting it," he said.

"But you evidently see my point. This man, Sid Kelso, must have a considerable amount of intelligence in addition to being a murderer. He is smart enough to know that we would not have come to Platte City alone. Murdering us will not solve that problem for him. Only by watching Stacy or me has he any chance of getting this information. Therefore, he cannot afford to harm her—or me—at least, for the time being. What I am trying to say is that we don't want you to take any unnecessary risks."

"I am going with him," Stacy said.

Her mother came close and caressed her. "You would only be a handicap to him, dear. Don't make his task more difficult. You are a woman. You know what I'm talking about. Partings are often sad enough, but they can be made even harder to bear. He *must* go out there. I see that now. We can't wait for this Kelso person to move against us. We must move first—before he can plan anything."

Stacy looked at him. Her eyes were glistening. "Come back!" she said. "Please come back! Nothing else really matters."

14

Early the following morning Vance walked to a livery in a back street and rented a horse.

"I'm on the look for a riding job," he told the hostler. "Where would I have the best luck?"

"Not much doin' right now with calf brand an' first beef gather over an' fall roundup weeks away," the hostler said. "I'd say the Fiddleback or the Bow'n Arrow. They're on the north trail. Can't miss 'em. You aimin' on keepin' thet horse out overnight?"

"Not if I can help it," Vance said. "Is there anything west where they might take on a hand?"

"Not in a day's round trip," the man said. "Ain't anythin' close in that direction except the Blockhouse. Sid Kelso an' Mike Deavers never hired a hand to my knowledge. Do their own ridin'. They raise more prairie dogs than cattle. They don't believe in hard work, I reckon."

"Looks like it's the north trail for me," Vance said. "You say to just follow my nose and I'll hit this Fiddleback and Bow and Arrow outfits."

He rode the trail north out of town, but soon left it, swinging west across country until he came upon a much-used wagon road that led westward. He kept this to his right, preferring to follow timber and broken country, for there was always the chance he might encounter Sid Kelso on the wagon road, if Kelso happened to be returning to Platte City.

His guidepoint was the Needle Buttes. This landmark was a ridge crowned by rocky spines, which gave it the aspect of a prehistoric monster. Progress was slow, for he kept scanning the country ahead before showing himself. The livery horse was heavy-gaited with a mind that was in favor of returning to Platte City at every excuse.

It was past midafternoon when he emerged on a bench. Blockhouse Ranch stood a mile or more away in a broad draw that angled westward along the base of Needle Buttes. A stream followed the draw, its water glinting in the sun here and there. The right-of-way of the Union Pacific Railroad also used this route some two or three miles beyond the ranch.

At first glance, the ranch had the appearance of being deserted. It suffered from neglect. A pioneer-style blockhouse squatted a short distance from an oblong, unpainted, shingled-roofed structure, so ugly that it could only have once been the barracks for troops. Beyond were a barn and three other sagging structures. Half a dozen horses grazed in a field, and two mounts were held in a corral near the barn.

He left his horse under cover and moved to a vantage point among boulders. The faint stain of smoke showed above a rusty chimney that jutted from the west end of the main building. A man carrying a water pail appeared, replenished the pail at a pool that was formed by blocking the tributary of the main stream. He returned to the house.

Time passed. The sun was hot. Eye flies danced tantalizingly. A hawk was an apparently motionless dot above the buttes. Vance shifted position occasionally and slapped at gnats.

Finally, two men left the house. They got saddle gear from a shed, went to the corral, roped horses, rigged and mounted. One was the lean, box-shouldered Sid Kelso. There was no mistaking his posture even at that distance. Vance surmised that Kelso's companion, heavy-legged and paunchy, must be Big Mike Deavers.

The pair headed in his direction, but remained on the bottom of the draw and passed by at half-a-mile distance. They vanished east into the breaks of the country. They were avoiding the wagon road, and their general direction was toward Platte City.

Vance debated whether to follow them. However, it was little more than an hour's ride to town, and there was still at least three hours of daylight left. Blockhouse Ranch lay temptingly before him, evidently deserted. The smoke from the chimney had faded long since. The livery hostler had said that Sid Kelso and his partner were usually the only persons at the ranch. And, as Amanda Fitzroy had said, there was little likelihood of danger for herself or Stacy in broad daylight.

There was in him the driving belief that the stolen beef money was hidden at this ranch. A chance to investigate might never come again. He returned to his horse, mounted and circled the ranch so as to appear that he had come riding up the wagon trail from Platte City.

He turned down the short, weed-grown spur road, passed the weathered blockhouse which evidently had not been entered for years, and rode into the ranch yard.

"Anybody home?" he called out.

The place remained silent. Convinced it was deserted, he dismounted and looped the reins of the horse over a gnawed tie rail in the shade of a tree. There were three doors to the long former barracks, all facing in the same direction, which was upon the corrals and barn and sheds. These stood on what had been the parade ground of the past.

The farthest doors to his right were nailed shut and weeds had overgrown their steps. The nearest door entered what evidently was the kitchen. This door was unlocked. He opened it and stepped in.

Used dishes were scattered on a plank table which bore a worn, grease-caked oilcloth cover.

A blackened wood range still gave out heat. A big, soot-stained coffeepot stood at the back of the stove.

He explored the building. Only about a third of the long structure was being used. Plank partitions had been built, forming a hallway which gave access to two bedrooms. A door at the end of the hallway opened into the remaining echoing space of the structure, which was a gloomy catch-all, cluttered with empty packing cases, wolf and bear traps and the general accumulation of the years. Windows, coated with dust and cobwebs, gave gray light.

A brass bedstead graced one bedroom. The other merely had a bedspring and mattress resting on the floor. Both rooms were unkempt. These evidently were the sleeping quarters of Sid Kelso and his partner.

A locomotive whistle sounded in the distance. From a window in the kitchen Vance saw a freight train heading eastward toward Platte City on the Union Pacific tracks.

He saw that a shack adjoining the barn served as a blacksmith shop. He left the main house and walked to the shack. Its interior was blackened by the forge smoke of years, but the forge was cold and apparently had not been used in some time. Alongside the shack was the scrap pile—a sizable heap of discarded, rusty horseshoes, broken wagon tires and wagon hounds and reaches.

Also in the scrap heap was railroad iron—broken lengths of rails and rods, heavy bolts and even a sizable chunk of a freight car wheel. Vance surmised that this was salvage from some railroad wreck that must have taken place in the vicinity long in the past.

He rocked on his bootheels while he inspected the heap. This, he felt certain, was from where the weighty contents of the substitute express boxes had come. He singled out rusty "chairs" bearing the RIC initials that he had found in the boxes in Roy Carvell's barn.

He straightened, then bent over to brush out the heelprints his boots had made in the soot-blackened earth. He heard a step behind him.

He started to whirl, snatching for his six-shooter. He was too late. He had a glimpse of a man leaping at him, swinging a club at his head. He knew this man.

He could not escape the blow. It crashed on his head, and he was engulfed in a paralyzing blast of pain. He reeled and slumped to the black earth, his pistol still only half-drawn.

He fought his way back to consciousness. He was still drugged by a monumental inertia that he had failed time after time to shake off.

Slowly, painfully, he finally became really alive. He realized that the blackness that engulfed him was real. It was night. At first he had thought he was blind, but he knew now that he must have lain here for hours.

He tried to move and discovered that his wrists were tied at his back. His ankles were also lashed together. His shirt had been ripped from him, and his six-shooter and holster were gone. Memory returned.

Light struck his eyes, dazzling him. A door had been opened. The light came from a lamp in the hands of someone who was only a shadow. He discovered that he was lying in the cluttered storage room in the ranch building.

The toe of a boot roughly probed his ribs. "Wakin' up, huh?" a jeering voice spoke. The shadow came closer. A face materialized. The face of Len Kelso.

"You know somethin'," Len said. "You was the last jigger in the world I figured would be in on this. The very damned last one."

Len bent closer. He was grinning. He had been drinking whisky and was unshaven, his eyes bloodshot, but he was savagely triumphant.

He grasped Vance by the hair, shaking him roughly. "Just how did them high-toned Fitzroys come to pick a man fresh out of the pen to come up here an' do their snoopin'? That's what I want to know."

Vance tried to sit up, and failed. "I should have expected that you'd show up here, Len," he mumbled.

"I got here a couple of days ago," Len said. "To visit my brother."

"And to see that you got your slice of the Del Rosa beef money," Vance said.

Len continued to grin. "What beef money?"

"I had a hunch that night in Del Rosa that I should know that fellow who called himself Ed Walsh," Vance said. "There's a resemblance. So you're brothers?"

"Me'n Sid used to be pardners in this place," Len said. "I got into a scrape a few years back, an' had to cut out. I went to Texas."

"That was quite a thing you fellows pulled," Vance said. "Whose idea was it? Yours?"

Len fell for the flattery and talked boastfully. "Me an' Harv Lemmon an' the barn boss of the stage division at Buffalo Bend worked a flim-flam a few years ago, tradin' off an express box filled with junk for a money shipment. But the laugh was on us that time, fer there was only a couple hundred dollars in the box. In copper pennies, fer Gawd's sake. We throwed the blasted things in the river."

"This time it paid off a little better," Vance commented.

"You said it. Sid recalled that stunt when old Ironpants Fitzroy made that ten-strike here with the Del Rosa pool herd. He talked Harv Lemmon an' Tim Murphy into goin' into it ag'in with him. It worked slick as a willow whistle. There ain't

234

nobody that knows we got that jag o' double-eagles. That is, nobody except maybe you an' Stacy Fitzroy."

"Where've you got it, Len? Here at the ranch?"

Len's mood changed. "That's for me to know," he said uglily.

"You can't spend it, you know. It's marked money."

"We kin wait. There'll be other double-eagles from that mint showin' up sooner or later. Only a few of us know the beef money's still up here. We won't tell, will we?"

"Neither will Harvey Lemmon nor Tim Murphy," Vance said. "Nor Roy Carvell."

"Shut up!" Len snarled. "They brung it on theirselves. Harv Lemmon tried to shake us down for more'n his share. Tim Murphy got to drinkin' too much. He might have talked. An' the same with Roy."

"It was Sid who took care of Lemmon and Tim Murphy, wasn't it? I happened to have been in Buffalo Bend that night and saw Sid ride away. I couldn't place him at the time, but I knew I'd seen him somewhere before. I'd played poker with him in Del Rosa. He used the name of Ed Walsh. First, he took care of Harv Lemmon, then rode to Buffalo Bend that same night and shot Tim Murphy. He worked fast. He must have been only a day or so ahead of me on the trip here from Del Rosa."

"Sid headed for San'tone not long after we sandbagged old Ironpants," Len boasted. "He came here by train. I hung around Del Rosa about a week before clearin' out."

"Just why did you pick on Roy Carvell to get mixed up in this thing?"

Len slapped his thigh and snickered. The more he drank the more talkative he was becoming. "We needed somebody with a strong back an' a weak mind. Them boxes was too heavy for two men to handle in a hurry. We also wanted a meetin' place away from my ranch. If things went wrong we aimed on lettin' Roy take care of it while we made tracks. Roy was dumb. He was so dumb it was pitiful. He fell fer pullin' that stage stickup a couple years ago, didn't he? I never had no intention o' bein' on that stage, but I would have cut in for my share if Roy had got away with any real money. I never could figure why you took the blame for that holdup."

"I had my reasons," Vance said.

"Roy fell for what I told him this time too. You ought to have seen his face when he found them boxes was full of junk. It was all I could do to keep from bustin' out laughin'."

"Exactly why did you and Sid take the risk of stealing those boxes at Oak Hill?"

"It was what you might call an inspiration. Sid had come down to Del Rosa to see what happened when Ironpants found out what was really in them boxes. Ironpants had never laid eyes on him, so he was safe enough. Sid knew I was livin' down in the Del Rosa. He hadn't really thought of stealin' them dummy boxes, but it looked like a sure-fire way to set up a blind trail. So we did it. They're lookin' for the money down there. It was a real smart thing, if I do say it myself."

"It was Sid who sneaked back to Whisky Ford and found that Roy Carvell was still alive, wasn't it?" Vance asked. "So he took care of that little matter while you set up an alibi for yourself."

Len's air of joviality vanished again, and for good. He drove his boot again into Vance's ribs, adding a new misery to the pain that still throbbed in his head.

"You're doin' a lot o' talkin' out o' turn!" Len snarled. "Just how come you got mixed up in this?"

"I wonder myself," Vance said.

"I reckon Roy Carvell told you a lot of things," Len said. "Maybe that ten percent reward that old Ironpants set up looked good to you. After Sid recognized that purty hash slinger in town last night as none other than Stacy Fitzroy, we knew she hadn't come up here alone. So Sid told me to hang around here an' stay under cover today in case somebody came snoopin' around the ranch. Shore enough, somebody did. You could have knocked me over with a chicken feather when I saw who it was."

A new thought chilled Vance. Stacy! And her mother! "What time is it?" he asked.

"Goin' on midnight, not that it makes any difference to you," Len snarled. "You been layin' there for hours. I was beginnin' to think I'd tapped you a leetle too hard."

"That's real thoughtful of you to worry about me, Len."

"Wasn't it?" Len said. "Fact is I was lonesome. I wanted someone to talk to. You are the one."

He went to the kitchen and returned with a steaming coffee mug and a jug of whisky. He sloshed whisky into the coffee, tested it and took a drink.

"Where did Sid and Big Mike Deavers go?" Vance asked. "I saw them heading east late this afternoon."

"To town, where else?" Len said. "To bring back a package."

The chill increased in Vance. "Package?"

The whisky was blurring Len's tongue, but not the savagery of his eyes. "A purty package. Done up in petticoats."

"What are you driving at?"

"You know who I'm talkin' about?" Len snarled. "Stacy Fitzroy, that's who. Sid aims to fetch her out to the ranch. They ought to be showin' up before long."

"Why would they want to bring her here?"

Len stared at him coldly. "For one thing, to ask her a few questions."

"About what?"

"We want to find out if anyone else came to Platte City with you two. You can be the first to answer that question—an' it better match up with the one she gives. Who else came with you?"

"Nobody, of course," Vance said.

Once more he received a kick in the ribs. It drove the breath from him in a gust of agony. "You're lyin'," Len said. "But you'll talk. Or she will." He added, "If she's able to talk."

Vance was silent. Len went back to the kitchen to replenish his coffee mug, leaving Vance torn by guilt and self-accusation. He had underestimated his opposition and had walked into a trap. A trap that would be fatal for him and Stacy. And for Amanda Fitzroy.

The Kelsos believed there was sure to be a third party on their trail, or perhaps more, but Len, at least, was unaware of the presence of Amanda Fitzroy in Platte City.

Len evidently had not believed Vance was in physical condition to be dangerous and had been careless in binding his wrists. The knot slipped a trifle when Vance tested it with main strength— not enough to free his hands, but to offer a faint glimmer of hope at least.

Len returned with his mug of coffee and again

added whisky. "I kin hardly wait to see the purty package," he leered. "I shore hope nothin' happens to her."

"Where's the money?" Vance asked.

Lance cursed him and lifted a boot to kick him once more. He decided against it. "You got a nerve, Jardine," he said grudgingly. "I guess you know what yo're in for, don't you?"

Vance wanted to keep Len talking. "I'll make you a little bet," he said. "I say that money is hid out close to where we are right now. Right in this house, maybe."

"Even if I told you, it wouldn't do you no good," Len said.

"If that's the way it's going to be, there's no reason why I should tell you anything you want to know, now is there?" Vance said.

"You'll tell. You or Stacy Fitzroy. There're ways of loosin' yore tongues."

"Maybe it won't do you any good to know where the money is either, Len. It didn't do Harvey Lemmon nor Tim Murphy any good, did it?"

Len glowered at him. "Shut up before I kick yore teeth in. Me an' Sid are splittin'—"

He broke off, deciding he was saying too much. But Vance believed he had the answer. Big Mike Deavers apparently was slated for the same fate as had overtaken the other partners of the Kelsos.

Len stamped back to the kitchen. Vance tore at his bonds, and his wrists came free. Before he could take any advantage of that effort Len returned. This time he was carrying the big, grease-blackened coffeepot. It was steaming and he was using potholders to protect his hands.

He stood over Vance with the receptacle poised. "How 'bout a little cawfee, Jardine?" he said. "It's good an' hot. Boilin' hot!"

He tilted the pot with torturing deliberation. A small spurt of the scalding liquid spilled from the spout. Vance tried to roll aside in an attempt to avoid the torture. He escaped the majority of the liquid but enough struck his bare chest to drive new agony through him.

Len guffawed. "Now that's no way to waste good cawfee, Jardine. Next time I'll see to it that you swaller it. All I want is for you to answer one question. Did anybody else come to Platte City from the Del Rosa with you an' the purty package?"

Another spurt of scalding liquid descended, this time toward Vance's face. Again he managed to jerk his head aside in time to escape the worst of it, but his cheek was seared by scalding drops.

"There's nobody else," he gritted.

"Just you an' Stacy Fitzroy, hey?" Len jeered. "Just you an' her came all the way up here together to snoop around. Now that was real cozy, wasn't it? Why, you jailbird, do you reckon

I'd believe she'd have anythin' to do with you? She, or whoever's with her, hired you because they know you're tough. You can handle a gun a leetle too well, if you ask me. I've seen you win prize money with a six. Now it ain't worth the misery you're bringin' on yoreself to be mule-headed. Who's with you an' her? Talk, or the next time I'll make mighty sure you git a swaller or two of this cawfee in yore gullet. Who is he?"

Lying on the floor, Vance heard sounds, communicated by the earth. Horses were approaching. He again stalled desperately for time. Help might be coming.

"If I told you, what then?" he asked.

Len guffawed. "Why, I'll just turn you loose, o' course. What else? Talk or—"

Kelso now also became aware that riders were near. He set aside the coffeepot, picked up the lamp and hurried into the kitchen, closing the door behind him, leaving Vance in darkness.

The horses came into the ranch yard and were yanked to a stop. Men's voices sounded. Boots clumped on the kitchen floor. More voices. Len Kelso began laughing coarsely.

Another voice: "Keep your filthy hands off me!"

Vance felt icily empty and defeated. That was Stacy! They had her! They had brought her here, a prisoner!

15

The door to the storeroom opened. Figures crowded in. Len carried the lamp. Stacy was held between Sid Kelso and Big Mike Deavers. Deavers had a thick black mustache and a week's growth of porcupine black beard on his heavy jowls. He had wicked, small eyes, set beneath bushy brows.

Stacy tried to scream when she saw Vance lying on the dusty floor, his ankles bound, his wrists apparently still tied at his back. Sid Kelso had anticipated that and broke off the outcry by clapping a hand roughly over her mouth.

"Keep your mouth shut, susie," he warned. "Talk only when I tell you to. Yellin' won't do you no good anyway. Ain't nobody within miles what could hear you."

He added, "Folks wouldn't be interested, anyway. It wouldn't be the first time ladies have been heard at night at Blockhouse."

Vance kept his hands clasped at his back, praying they would not inspect his bonds. To divert them, he spoke to Stacy.

"What happened?"

"I left the Palace by the back door," she said. "They were waiting for me in the darkness. They

243

told me they'd kill me if I screamed. I think they meant it. They made me put on a man's hat and a slicker and ride with them through the back streets out of town."

Sid Kelso bent close, peering at Vance. "Say, ain't you the jigger I played poker with that night in Del Rosa?"

"I wouldn't be surprised if I was," Vance said.

"So that's how you got onto me?" Kelso said, thinking it over. "Maybe you seen me in town an' found out my name was Kelso. Was that it?"

"You do the guessing," Vance said. "I'm just lying around."

"What's happened to your face? It's red as raw beef."

Len spoke. "I was askin' him if there was anybody else in this, except the little petticoat here. I was offerin' him a leetle hot cawfee to loosen his tongue."

"What did he say?"

"I had just started to work on him when you an' Mike pulled in."

"Did you say this fellow is an ex-con?"

"That's right. He was sent up for a stage stickup down Del Rosa way. He didn't actually do it, but took the blame. It's quite a story. I'll tell you all about it later."

Sid turned to Stacy. "Why did you git a jailbird to help you?"

She shrugged. She must be aware that the Kelsos did not intend to let her live much longer, but she had control of her emotions. "What does it matter?" she said. "He's here. So am I."

"And who else is around?" Sid asked silkily.

"There's no one else," she said. She was refusing to quail or show fear of these men.

Vance met her eyes. She smiled at him, warmly, intimately, as though they shared a great secret. He was uplifted to sublime heights. She was telling him she loved him.

Len Kelso was speaking. "Maybe I kin think o' ways to persuade her to talk."

"Now, you don't want to give Len that pleasure, do you, dearie?" Sid said to her. "He seems to think he'll enjoy it."

"I shore would," Len snarled. "She never acted like I was fit to be alive. Used to look right through me, as though I wasn't even there. I'll make her know I'm a human bein'. I'll make her beg."

Vance spoke. "I'll lay you odds that will never happen, Len. A hundred to one. A thousand to one."

"Shut up!" Len yelled. He seized the coffeepot and would have resumed the torture on Vance, but his brother restrained him. "Take it easy!" Sid warned. "He can't talk if he's dead."

"How can either of us tell you anything when there's nothing to tell?" Vance said. "There's nobody else."

His eyes again met those of Stacy. He knew she understood that the Kelsos did not know her mother was in Platte City. They were assuming that, if there was a third person, it must be a man. He and Stacy shared a bitter, grim pact. Protect Amanda! Vance, his hands virtually free, forced himself to wait.

The three men were spread around him at the moment so there would be little hope of bringing on anything more than a hopeless battle in which he would be killed. That would mean Stacy's death also, preceded by torture in an attempt to make her talk. Looking at her, he saw the strength of her virtue, the immovable will to protect her mother from these men.

Len looked eagerly at his brother. Sid shrugged, and nodded. Len set the lamp on an empty packing case and again picked up the coffeepot, with its still-scalding contents. "Take off her clothes," he said.

Big Mike Deavers spoke for the first time. "Hold on!" he protested. "I didn't figger on anythin' like this."

"Well, well!" Sid said caustically. "What's in your craw, Mike?"

"Sometimes you git worse'n the noose fer botherin' women," Deavers said. "I seed what they done to a feller up at Divide a time back. They drug him, feet-first, through rocks an' brush at the end o' a ketch rope. Then they hung him over a slow fire 'til he was screamin' fer them to kill—"

"Yo're yella, Mike!" Len howled.

"I'm yella when it comes to bein' slow-burned over a fire," Deavers said. "Another time, up on Wind River, I seed 'em stake a man down in a nest o' rattlers, then teasin' the snakes 'til they got riled up. He'd touched a woman."

Len roughly shouldered Deavers aside, grasped Stacy's dress, with the intention of ripping it from her. He paused. His brother and Deavers went motionless, listening. Vance heard it, also. Wheels were grinding on the spur road, approaching the ranch house.

The voice of a woman hailed the place. "Anybody to home? I'm lost an' needin' directions."

The voice, although quavering and meant to give the impression of age and helplessness, belonged to Amanda Fitzroy.

Sid Kelso muttered an oath. "Go out there, Mike, an' see who'n blazes she is an' what she wants," he murmured.

He bent and jammed a six-shooter against Vance's chest. "If either you or the girl makes a peep, you're both dead," he warned. "Keep your traps closed."

Deavers tramped through the kitchen into the ranch yard. "What do you want?" he spoke, his voice carrying. "Who air you?"

"I'm Emmy Peters, tryin' to find my son's

place somewhere around here," Amanda Fitzroy said tremulously. "I must have took the wrong fork some place. Kin you tell me how to git to his ranch. His name is George Peters."

"Never heerd o' him, lady," Deavers rumbled. "There ain't no ranches fer fifteen miles or more west o' here an' none of 'em air owned by anybody of that name."

"Oh, my land!" Amanda shrilled in her assumed voice. "I jest don't know what to do. I'm about tuckered, an' so is my horse. You got any womenfolk I kin talk to?"

"Ain't no women here," Deavers said. "You better head back to Platte—"

He went silent for a moment. "Say!" he exclaimed. "Ain't that buggy the one that belongs to Sim Dutton who owns the Palace Cafe in town? What are you doin' with—?"

Amanda spoke. Her voice was no longer falsetto. It was tense and very grim. "Put up your hands and turn around. Just stand there, or I'll put a bullet through your fat carcass."

The two Kelso brothers were so startled, their heads turned. Vance seized the only chance he might have. He did not know why Amanda Fitzroy had come here alone, but she had diverted their attention for a moment.

He rolled over, came to a sitting position, his hands free. He pivoted, using his bound legs as a flail. They caught Len Kelso at the ankles, bowling him off his feet. Len instinctively tried to seize Stacy for support as he toppled, but she evaded him, darting out of reach.

In the same motion, Vance seized Sid Kelso at the knees in a plunging tackle, and sent him also crashing to the floor. Kelso tried to shoot as he fell, but Vance had anticipated that. He twisted his body aside, wrenching Kelso in the opposite direction so that the bullet went far wide, sending up a fog of dust from the floor where it struck yards away.

The bonds on Vance's ankles had loosened a trifle, but still clung, handicapping him. He doubled his legs and straightened them in a jackknife, driving both feet into Sid's face. That spun Kelso's body violently around and the six-shooter fell from his hand.

Vance hurled himself forward and managed to seize the weapon before Sid could recover it. Len Kelso landed on his back, flailing at him with the muzzle of his pistol. Vance plunged forward, head-over-heels, in a somersault that was helped by the momentum of Len's own plunge. Len landed on his back with Vance's weight descending on him. Len managed to tear free, but he was wheezing in agony, the breath driven from him.

Len began to swing his six-shooter around to shoot Vance at point-blank range. Stacy moved in, swinging the coffeepot. The scalding flood struck Len in the face, drenching him. He uttered a cry of pain. The sound rose to a choked scream of torment. He reeled back, clawing at his face, dropping his pistol.

Vance twisted around, the six-shooter in his hand. Sid snatched up the gun his brother had dropped. Vance was forced to hold his fire, for Stacy was in the line.

Sid brought the .45 to bear on Vance, the hammer eared back, but Stacy moved in and kicked his arm with the grace and skill of a dancer, sending the pistol sailing a dozen feet away. It exploded, but the bullet went harmlessly into the ceiling.

Sid dove to retrieve the weapon, and rolled into the shelter of the packing case on which the lamp stood. Vance put a bullet through the lamp. Kerosene and broken glass showered Kelso in his hiding place.

The wick, the flame guttering low, dangled over the side of the packing case, clung for a moment, then dropped to the floor. Except for that tiny, feeble flame there was no light in the room for seconds.

Vance heard Sid stumbling to new cover. The man, his clothing soaked in kerosene, had realized his danger. Vance sent a bullet in the direction of the sound. "Take cover, Stacy!" he shouted. "Duck! He's going to shoot!"

Kelso fired, but he was aiming only at the

sound of a voice, and missed. Vance seized an empty barrel and sent it spinning across the room to confuse his opponent.

The pool of kerosene on the floor burst into flames. Smoke fogged the room. Len Kelso staggered around, blinded and moaning, pleading with his brother to help him.

Vance seized Stacy's arm, heading her for the door, and went hopping after her on his bound legs. He sent another empty barrel spinning through the smoke to create confusion and fired three times in the general direction of Sid Kelso. That drove Sid to cover long enough for him to push Stacy into the kitchen and follow her.

She steadied him and they scrambled on through the kitchen and into the open starlight in the ranch yard. A six-shooter blasted as they emerged. Big Mike Deavers was reeling. He fell, clutching at his leg. Amanda Fitzroy stood beside the top buggy, her .45 still poised, a swirl of powder-smoke rising. The horse was rearing, frightened by the shooting.

"The fool!" Amanda said. "I told him I'd shoot if he tried to come at me. And I did it. It's his own fault."

"How did you get here, Mother?" Stacy chattered.

"I glimpsed them riding away with you. This rig was standing in front of the Palace, so I helped myself to it. I just followed my nose out the west trail until I saw this place. The blockhouse told me I'd come to the right ranch."

Mike Deavers lay groaning with a bullet-broken leg. "I only wanted to wing him," Amanda explained.

Vance managed to free his ankles. He seized the six-shooter in Deavers's holster and made sure it was loaded. He handed his own gun to Stacy. "There's only one good shell left in it," he said. "And no time to reload. Cover that far side. They might try to come out a window. Mrs. Fitzroy, you watch the far end. There's a window there too. Shoot at them. Drive them this way—toward the kitchen. I'll take care of them when they come out."

The windows of the long building were now crimson with the spreading fire inside. "Come out, Sid!" Vance shouted. "Hands high. Bring Len with you! You can't stay there much longer. Leave your gun in there!"

He heard window glass being smashed. Stacy fired a shot, the last she had in the gun, but the Kelsos did not know that. "I'll kill you if you try to come out that window!" she shouted. "Do what Vance Jardine tells you. Go out through the kitchen!"

Sid Kelso did not heed. Vance ran to the side Stacy was guarding just in time to see Sid come hurtling through the window, taking jagged glass and portions of the sash with him. Sid was a

252

flaming torch. He began to scream for help, but was beyond that. His agonized voice faded off. He rolled in the grass for a time, then lay still in death.

Len Kelso, still clutching his scalded face, came lurching out of the kitchen door into the open. Flames burst through the roof of the structure.

Stacy looked at Vance and said thinly, "I guess it's over, isn't it?" Then she crumpled to the ground in a dead faint.

Her mother came hurrying. "Are there any more of them?" she asked Vance. She still clutched the .45 with which she had shot Mike Deavers.

"No," Vance said. He ran his hand over his eyes. A trite question. A trite answer.

Amanda Fitzroy, who had been captain of her soul through all this, began to talk wildly. "Wasn't it good luck that Sim Dutton happened to leave his horse and buggy in front of the Palace tonight so that I could get here in time?"

Then Amanda sat down slowly in a state of complete exhaustion. The long building was burning fiercely, flames darting high in the air. Vance carried Amanda to safer distance, then returned to care for Stacy.

She was reviving however, and he helped her to her feet and held her until sure she was able to stand. "This is a hell of a time for you two to collapse," he said. "It's about all over!"

Len Kelso was still wandering around, moaning that he was blind. Vance caught his arm, halting him. "Where is it, Len?" he asked. "Where's the money? You're through! Finished! Sid is dead. Deavers has been shot. You might as well talk."

Len babbled incoherently. It was Mike Deavers who spoke. "I'm bleedin' bad, mister. Fix a bandage or somethin'. The money's buried in the stable in a box stall."

Stacy laughed hysterically. "Of course. Where else does anyone bury old express boxes whether they're filled with gold, or with the ghosts of murdered men, but in a box stall? We know where there are boxes buried down in the Del Rosa. We—"

Vance took her in his arms. "There now," he said. "There now. I tell you it's all over. We're all safe now."

She clung to him. "I love you!" she said. "I've always loved you. Do you love me? You must! You must!"

Amanda had revived. "Of course he loves you," she said. She took charge, trying to hide her mortification over her moment of weakness. "I'll take care of these two rascals until you find a wagon to pack them into town," she said. "I'm sure they'll stay alive that long, unfortunately."

Neither her daughter nor Vance replied. Vance was holding Stacy close in his arms and saying words to which she was listening with tearful happiness.

It was nearing midmorning when the three express boxes were finally brought to light. By that time Len Kelso and Big Mike Deavers were in the hospital in Platte City under guard.

Sheriff Buck Joseph was in charge of excavating the treasure. A considerable portion of the population of Platte City had arrived, and was looking on as Stacy and her mother opened the boxes and revealed the bags of gold coin that had been undisturbed since Web Fitzroy had counted the money before seeing it placed in the big safe at the Stockman's Bank.

Amanda was radiantly happy. Then a new thought suddenly dismayed her. "Good land of living!" she breathed. "Who is going to tell my husband that he guarded three boxes of trash without ever suspecting he'd been hoodwinked. Think of his pride!"

"Don't look at me," Vance said. "It's no job for a prospective son-in-law, now is it?"

Stacy spoke. "I would say, Mister Harding, that your prospects are very good."

| Books are produced in the United States using U.S.-based materials | Books are printed using a revolutionary new process called THINKtech™ that lowers energy usage by 70% and increases overall quality | Books are durable and flexible because of smythe-sewing | Paper is sourced using environmentally responsible foresting methods and the paper is acid-free |

Center Point Large Print
600 Brooks Road / PO Box 1
Thorndike, ME 04986-0001 USA

(207) 568-3717

US & Canada:
1 800 929-9108
www.centerpointlargeprint.com